JUSTICE LEAGUE

The Gauntlet

JUSTICE LEAGUE™

The Gauntlet

by

LOUISE SIMONSON

Based on a story idea
by Rich Fogel

BANTAM BOOKS
NEW YORK • TORONTO • LONDON • SYDNEY • AUCKLAND

THE GAUNTLET

A Bantam Book/October 2002

ISBN: 0-553-48773-6

Visit us on the Web! www.randomhouse.com/kids
Educators and librarians, for a variety of teaching tools, visit us at
www.randomhouse.com/teachers

Visit DC Comics at www.dccomics.com

Published simultaneously in the United States and Canada

Bantam Books is an imprint of Random House Children's Books, a division of
Random House, Inc. BANTAM BOOKS and the rooster colophon are registered
trademarks of Random House, Inc. Bantam Books, 1540 Broadway, New York,
New York 10036.

PRINTED IN THE UNITED STATES OF AMERICA

OPM   10 9 8 7 6 5 4 3 2 1

To Jenette Kahn,

constant champion of Wonder Woman

With thanks and admiration to William Moulton Marston, creator of Wonder Woman; to Mike Carlin, without whom I wouldn't be here; to Rich Fogel, for his challenging story outline; to Bruce Timm and his team at Warner Bros. Animation, for just the right "look"; to Juliana Muth, for past and present help; to Marissa Walsh, for her perceptive comments; and to Charles Kochman, whose insights and good humor make working with him a joy. —LS

CHAPTER
1

"**R**emember! We don't act until we know what we're up against!"

Wonder Woman brushed her long, dark, wind-blown hair from her eyes and grimaced, glancing over toward the dome of the National Gallery of Art, where Green Lantern and Hawkgirl perched, surveying the Washington, D.C., skyline. *GL is giving orders as usual,* Wonder Woman thought, *acting like the rest of us are rank amateurs.*

Their silhouettes were clear against the night sky, and she saw Hawkgirl ruffle her wing feathers in a half-insulted, half-amused gesture. "To do otherwise might make matters worse, Green Lantern. You don't need to teach me my business."

Through the communication device worn in her ear, Wonder Woman could tell that Hawkgirl's voice was chiding. Hawkgirl had been a top cop on her homeworld, Thanagar. She knew what she was doing.

Wonder Woman could also hear the murmuring voices of Superman, Batman, and Martian Manhunter. They were at the end of the long park known as the Mall, standing atop the Capitol Building, discussing the Justice League's options.

Batman had picked up vague rumors of a planned attack on Washington, which he had traced back to a member of Intergang, one of the human thugs allied with the other-dimensional ruler of the New Gods, Darkseid. Batman wasn't sure—none of them were sure—what was going to happen next. Or if *anything* would happen. But the members of the Justice League planned to counter any threat to the safety and security of the United States and its citizens.

From atop the roof of the cylindrical Hirshhorn Museum, Wonder Woman scanned the heavens.

The Flash crouched beside her, polishing off his first sizzling slice of ham, sausage, and pepperoni pizza, then reaching into the box for a second slice.

The red-suited superspeedster, who expended enormous amounts of energy when he ran, had to refuel constantly.

He bit into the gooey mound and yelped. "Hot! Hot! Yikes!" Then he glanced up at Wonder Woman. "Want some?"

"Hush!" Wonder Woman hissed. "I thought I saw something."

"Don't get your tiara in a twist, your royal highness!" Flash mumbled sarcastically, his mouth full. "With all humility, Princess Diana, you don't know what you're missing!"

I sounded like my mother in one of her stressed-out moods, Wonder Woman thought. *What's wrong with me?*

She stared intently into the night sky. Her people believed the stars held answers. She could use some now.

What am I doing here? she asked herself. *Exiled forever from the Amazons and Themyscira, our secret island home?*

She told herself it was her own choice to live here in what the Amazons called Man's World. She truly believed that the larger Earth needed her special abilities. And yet, away from the miraculous island of immortal warrior women and their queen, her mother ... without a place among her people, who was she?

As a child on Themyscira, Diana had once tried to hold water in the cupped palms of her hands. But no matter how tightly she pressed her fingers together, the water trickled away.

She was grown now, but she was clutching just as tightly to her Amazon identity, she thought. And, like the water, she felt it slipping through her fingers.

Out of the corner of her eye, Wonder Woman spotted a wavering shimmer in the starlight.

"There it is again! What is it?" She flew a few feet into the air, straining to get a closer look.

Flash grabbed the golden lasso that hung from a loop at her waist. "Wonder Woman! Wait!" he said.

She turned in midair and hissed. "Let go! There's something there!"

"Maybe to your goddess-like eyes, Princess, but I can't see—"

"Obviously," she whispered. "*You* see as humans see. But Darkseid is one of the New Gods and has the tricks of a god. And we *Amazons* deal with gods on a regular basis! Now let go!"

She jerked free and whirled up into the air.

"Ever hear of teamwork?" Flash began, but she was already gone. "Might as well save my breath to cool my pizza," he muttered to himself.

I know the Flash thinks I can be a royal pain, Wonder Woman thought as she flew up toward the faint shimmer. *I guess I can, but— Oh, how can I expect him to understand when I don't understand myself? This isn't what we planned, but how else can I be sure?*

Wonder Woman heard Superman speaking over the communicator. "Diana, what—?" His voice dissolved in a crackle of static.

"Superman?" she said. But he didn't seem to be able to hear her either.

Whatever is up there is interfering with League communications equipment, Wonder Woman thought. *I wonder—*

Then suddenly she slammed into an object that should not have been there.

For an instant it flickered into almost-visibility—an armored, brick-colored creature with rudimentary wings, holding a gleaming bomb-shaped canister as long as her arm. Its demonic, helmeted face snarled rage through inch-long fangs.

A jumble of monster voices surrounded her.

"We're cloaked!"

"How'd she see us?"

"Who cares! Destroy her—and get on with the mission!"

"Deliver the cylinder—"

Something struck her from behind, and for an instant, she was immobilized. Then she fell. Above her, the sky looked empty. But Wonder Woman had seen the monster. Smelled it. Knew its size and the faint sounds of its flight.

She fought off the paralysis, righted herself, and snatched her golden lasso from its catch at her waist. She whirled the rope overhead and flung it toward the spot where she expected the invisible monster to be.

The loop settled—and the rope went taut.

"Got you!" she muttered.

Energy blasts flew at her, apparently out of thin air. She held the rope tight with one hand and deflected the blasts with the bracelet on her other wrist. She heard muffled oaths and several screams as the ricocheting energy struck her assailants.

Serves them right! she thought grimly.

Suddenly, from all sides, invisible clawed hands

delivered a barrage of blows. The air reeked of monster breath.

There are dozens of them, she thought.

A blast of heat vision scythed upward from below, and a monster voice screamed, "It's Superman!"

Superman! Wonder Woman thought. Her struggle had taken mere seconds, but it had alarmed the League. They knew she was in trouble, even if they couldn't see the cause.

Wonder Woman jerked the rope with all her strength, pulling the invisible monster toward her.

He slammed into her. And again she saw him. *When I'm this close,* she reasoned, *I must be inside the invisibility field with him.*

The monster clutched the cylinder protectively. "Sorry, Charlie!" she growled, and wrenched it from the monster's hands.

"She has the Brain Binder!" a voice cried. "Get it!"

Another moaned, "No time! Superman's almost on us!"

A roaring vortex, appearing out of nowhere, encompassed them. "Desaad has sent a Boom Tube!" a gargoyle voice shouted. "Take her with us, back to Apokolips!"

Wonder Woman could barely hear their voices over

the roar that surrounded her. Invisible hands dragged her toward the vortex.

"We failed to deploy the Brain Binder!"

"But others will succeed!"

"Not a chance!" Wonder Woman yelled. Fighting the inexorable pull of the Boom Tube, she wrenched her arms free and hurled the canister downward.

"Superman!" she shouted. "Catch!"

Then, as the clamoring darkness enveloped her, she realized, *That might have worked—if the canister hadn't also been invisible!*

CHAPTER
2

Wonder Woman tumbled upward, as if she were being sucked into a tornado. She was too numb with shock to shake off the invisible assailants who clung to her throughout their interdimensional journey.

Then, with stomach-lurching suddenness, they emerged high in the air above a dark and sprawling megalopolis.

The churning Boom Tube disappeared.

Wonder Woman knew she wasn't in Washington anymore. The city below, partially visible through the sulfurous smog, was large, utilitarian, and completely without grace or beauty.

"Where am I?" she asked. *As if I can't guess,* she thought. *These creatures are Darkseid's minions.*

"Apokolips," snarled the voice beside her. "We have our orders. Lord Darkseid will welcome you personally to our great capital."

She glanced toward the voice. "What—who are you?" she asked.

"Parademons!" the Captain's voice said. "Reveal yourselves!"

As one, they became visible. Wonder Woman studied the gargoyle-like creatures speculatively. She might be able to overpower them, she thought, now that they no longer had the advantage of invisibility.

"Don't even consider it!" snarled the Captain. "You're outnumbered. In the blink of an eye I could call up hundreds more. We'd love to pound you into pulp. But I have orders to keep you whole—unless you try to escape."

"Try it!" snarled the monster chorus. "You made us fail Darkseid!"

"To fail Darkseid is to fail ourselves!" the Parademon she had lassoed earlier snarled, struggling ineffectively to free himself. "May Darkseid spare us long enough to destroy you!"

They dropped toward the city, toward a building so monumental that Wonder Woman thought it must be a palace. Then she saw the troops, serried ranks of armored figures goose-stepping with military precision down the wide avenues surrounding it. An army, she realized. The building below was no palace, but a vast fortress.

In the center of the roof below, a huge skylight slid open. The Parademons dragged her through it, into a stone-walled room draped with tapestries. They landed before a massive man seated on a marble throne. His craggy gray face looked as if it had been carved from granite. Wonder Woman would have thought him a statue except for his eyes, which held a flinty intelligence and the unyielding certainty of his own vast power. His watchful stillness contained lurking menace.

The Parademons fell prostrate, and with the guttural command "Bow before Great Darkseid!" they dragged Wonder Woman down with them. Some slammed on top of her, crushing her to the floor, to make certain she obeyed.

"Lord! We have shamed ourselves!" the Parademon Captain said. "We have lost the Brain Binder! But we have brought the woman who thwarted your plan! Punish us, Great Darkseid, as you see fit!"

Wonder Woman had heard enough. She jerked

upward, knocking aside the groveling Parademons, and stood. "Abase yourselves if you wish, you cringing gargoyles. But Wonder Woman, Amazon Princess of Themyscira, bows before no man! Nor will she long remain his prisoner."

She vaulted into the air, toward the skylight. She heard a yelp of rage and felt a jerk at the end of her lasso. Glancing back, she saw the furious Parademon still struggling to escape the loop that encircled it.

Darkseid raised a finger, and iron shutters abruptly covered the skylight as if the palace itself obeyed his every whim.

Wonder Woman whirled in midair, feeling the first stirrings of alarm.

Darkseid scowled at the Parademons. "That is the second time you've lost control of her," he said. His eyes began to glow red.

The Parademons gazed up at Darkseid, their faces suffused with terror. "The Omega Beam! Sire! No—"

A red glow surrounded and consumed the Parademon dangling at the end of Wonder Woman's lasso. It screamed in agony; then it was gone. The loop of her lasso fell limp and empty.

Wonder Woman gaped. The remaining Parademons

flattened themselves against the floor, afraid to make any sound or movement that might focus Darkseid's further wrath on them. But Darkseid, his curiosity piqued, ignored the cringing monsters as he eyed the lasso speculatively.

"Land, Wonder Woman!" he commanded.

Wonder Woman knew she was trapped, the prisoner of a being who could destroy with a glance. Her lasso was invulnerable. It was a creation of the goddess Hera, spun from her own girdle and protected with her magic. But Wonder Woman knew that complete invulnerability did not extend to her own body.

She landed.

She was tall, even for an Amazon, and her bearing was royal. She looked Darkseid in the eye. "It seems that, for now, Darkseid, I am your prisoner."

"Desaad, step forward!" Darkseid rumbled.

A hooded and robed man sidled up from behind a tapestry. He was thin and wiry with a sly, narrow face. He studied Wonder Woman with cruel, greedy eyes. His tongue flicked, snakelike, over his bottom lip.

He reached out to stroke her cheek. "Exquisite, Sire! Perfection itself! Give her to me, Lord," he murmured. "Let me break her for you!"

Wonder Woman felt her skin crawl. She grabbed Desaad's arm and tossed him across the room. "Touch me, and it is you who will be broken!"

"Brave words," Desaad snarled as he struggled to his feet. "Let us see how brave you truly are!"

He tossed a glowing ball at Wonder Woman. It unraveled into writhing strips that wrapped themselves around her face and body. Her red-and-gold armored breastplate protected her ribs, but the strands snaked up over her neck and face and around her bare arms and legs.

She flexed, trying to break them, but the more she struggled, the more tightly they bound her.

Darkseid glanced at the hooded figure. "You overstep your authority, Desaad," he said. "You deployed that squadron. They failed in their mission. Worse than failed. Would you share that Parademon's fate?"

Desaad cringed backward. "Your pardon, Sire. I thought only of your security. It must be as you desire! But we may yet recover the canister. And snatch from this apparent defeat a far greater victory."

Wonder Woman's bonds had grown so tight now, she could hardly breathe. "What was in that canister?" she croaked. "What is a Brain Binder?"

Desaad smirked. "The Brain Binder is a sophisti-cated neurological weapon that I devised—"

A neurological weapon? Wonder Woman had acted instinctively in taking the canister, but in doing so, she had saved innocent people from a horrible fate. Though she had paid a high price, she couldn't be sorry.

"You were going to release this weapon in Washington?" Wonder Woman gasped. "Why? To sub-vert America's government?"

"Great Darkseid has another, vaster aim," Desaad answered. "Such sabotage would be a useful side ef-fect, allowing us to more easily extend our control over—"

"Enough!" Darkseid's voice cracked like a whip.

Desaad cringed, and for a moment, he was silent. Then he whispered, "Lord, she will make a most in-triguing subject to study. Let me Bind her to you!"

"No!" Wonder Woman didn't know exactly how a Brain Binder worked, but she recognized the threat in Desaad's voice. She struggled and the restraint slid up to cover her nose and mouth.

Her head whirled, and her eyesight dimmed as she heard Darkseid say, "Take her, Desaad. That rope of hers withstood my Omega Beam. I want to know how. Test it, and her armor as well. Test *her*. Learn exactly where she came from, what her powers are, what protects her! I want to know everything about her that there is to know! Only then will I allow this 'Wonder Woman' to be broken and Bound to me!"

CHAPTER

3

Someone's screaming. Have to save them.

Wonder Woman struggled toward consciousness, but her eyelids felt as if they had been glued shut. She couldn't stand, could hardly move.

I must be dreaming, trapped in a nightmare of howls and stinks and darkness crowded with monsters. I'll be okay if I can just wake up, she told herself. *I have to wake up!* The scream reached a crescendo. Then, abruptly, it stopped.

The sudden silence shocked her into awareness. She was lying on rough-hewn stones that dug into her back. Her heart was pounding and she gulped great shuddering breaths. Her throat was sore and raw.

Was that me? she thought. *Was* I *screaming? But . . . why? Where am I?*

In an act of will, she forced her eyes open. Gloomy light seeped through a tiny, barred window and revealed her surroundings—a classic dungeon cell.

What am I doing here? she asked herself.

Memory surfaced slowly, like a goldfish in a murky pond.

The dungeon cell was in the manor belonging to Darkseid's minion Desaad. And the vile Desaad was preparing to study her as if she were a lab specimen—before he destroyed her mind and stole her will.

Wonder Woman fought down her panic, practicing the meditative breathing she had learned on Themyscira. Her mind must be free of fear and focused on her surroundings, on finding a way out.

She struggled to sit upright.

The barred window was set into a sturdy-looking metal door that would be her only hope of escape, once she freed herself from her wrist shackles. Oddly, they were bound to the wall, not by chains, but by a tangle of thick wires.

It figured somehow. Apokolips was, after all, a high-tech world. These were probably power shackles.

Not that it matters. Neither wires nor chains can hold Wonder Woman, she thought. *These, at least, I can break!*

She pulled at the wires. Nothing happened. But that was impossible. She was innately strong, and her magic armor amplified her own power tenfold. It allowed her to hold her own, even against Superman!

Her *armor*!

Wonder Woman looked down and saw, shocked, that she was now dressed in rags. Her glorious red-and-gold armor, her silver bracelets, and her unbreakable golden lasso were gone.

Once more her panic rose and this time she gave it full sway, letting adrenaline surge through her body to fuel her struggles. But without the aid of her armor, she still couldn't break her bonds.

Then, with a metallic clank, the cell door slid open. A hulking guard lurched into the cell, holding a cracked jar and a fist-sized gray cube.

He tossed the cube into her lap. "Energy Block," the man grunted. "Water too. Desaad must want to keep you alive for a while." He put down the jar. "Pullin' at them wires won't do no good. Only old Himon ever escaped this prison in one piece."

Keep him talking, Wonder Woman told herself. *Find out what you can.*

"Who—?" The question caught in her parched throat. She reached for the jar, gulped water, and tried again. "Who's Himon?"

"Nobody *you'll* ever meet," the guard snarled. "My name's Kranx. An' *mine's* the last face you'll ever see. Except for Desaad's."

He shuffled out the door.

Five levels above, in a laboratory packed with looming machinery, Desaad glanced at the video screen that was to be his private peep show into Wonder Woman's psyche. He licked his lips in anticipation, waiting for her flood of memories to begin.

And then he sighed.

Wonder Woman is testing her bonds, he thought impatiently. *Again.* The unexpected delay was making him edgy.

He studied the row of dials that measured her energy output and other physical data and smiled sourly. Without her armor, she had as much chance of breaking her bonds as he apparently had of breaking her lasso.

Desaad had been running Wonder Woman's lasso, armor, and bracelets through a series of experiments. He knew these artifacts enhanced her strength and speed and allowed her to fly. But, he had discovered, they had no effect on anyone else.

The armaments were powered by an as yet unknown energy: what this Amazon savage would probably call *magic*. Desaad didn't believe in magic. He was certain that once he had acquired sufficient data, he would be able to manipulate and exploit the power of her armor. And of Wonder Woman herself.

It was only a matter of time.

Slumped against the dungeon wall, Diana picked up the Energy Block. It looked, felt, and even smelled like a moldy sponge. But she would need all her strength to escape.

She bit into the cube and nearly gagged. It tasted as bad as it looked, but it was apparently what passed as nourishment, at least in this dungeon. Quickly she washed the morsel down with another swig of water.

Impulsiveness had gotten her captured, she

thought. Her quickness of perception and reaction. *No*, she admitted. *I have to be honest, at least with myself.*

Diana *could* have signaled the others. She'd had time. But she hadn't been sure of what she'd seen. And she didn't want to look unprofessional in front of Green Lantern and Superman and the rest of the Justice League. And so she had acted alone.

And, she remembered, not for the first time either. . . .

THE ARMOR

Princess Diana stares up at the stars that twinkle above Themyscira. Except for Diana, the city of Amazons surrounding her mother's palace is asleep. So only Diana sees the ball of fire streak soundlessly toward the invisible Dome of Magic, set in place by the gods to protect Themyscira.

The asteroid—if that is what it is—hits the dome and explodes silently. And Diana sees the afterimage of a giant tripod shape.

Should I sound the alarm? *Diana wonders as a*

second missile strikes the dome. Should I wake my mother and the others? Isn't this proof that the Earth is under attack by alien forces?

But her goddess-mother knows about the attacks. And her reaction is predictable—the gods will protect Themyscira. She would see those explosions as proof of their magical aid. She would tell Diana, once again, that whatever happens beyond Themyscira's borders is not the Amazons' concern, and she would order Diana not to take any action.

"Themyscira remains at peace—for now!" Diana mutters rebelliously. "But the human world beyond, what the Amazons call Man's World, is fighting for survival. And if Man's World is destroyed, how long will Themyscira remain unscathed?"

Diana has been trained to be a champion of a land that needs no protection, she thinks. It is Man's World that needs her abilities. Despite her mother's commands, Diana decides that she will aid humanity. But what can one Amazon do—even a superbly skilled Amazon? How can she even reach Man's World in time to help?

Diana gazes toward the Temple of Athena, Goddess of Wisdom and War.

And in a flash of insight, she has her answer.

Diana stands in the temple sanctuary. The giant statue of Athena gazes serenely down at her. Despite her disobedience to her mother, Diana feels she has Athena's blessing.

At the statue's feet lies the Sacred Armor of the Amazons, reserved for use by their champion in times of crisis—a red-and-gold breastplate that enhances the strength of the wearer and gives her the power of flight, silver bracelets that can deflect any weapon, and an indestructible golden lasso.

In peaceful Themyscira, these magic implements have never been worn. Until now.

Diana picks up the lasso.

"Mother, forgive me!" she whispers, then reaches for the breastplate.

"If you could see me chained here in this dungeon, Mother, would you smile and say, 'I told you so'?" Diana murmured.

Well, she probably wouldn't *smile.* Diana's loss of the armor was devastating. Not just for what the armor was, but for what it represented. No, her mother would be disappointed in her once again.

Not since she was very small had Diana felt like she was the perfect daughter her mother had longed for. And after a while she had stopped *trying* to be, had even taken a guilty pleasure in matching wits with a mother whose will was at least as strong as her own.

CHAPTER 4

"**S**o, Wonder Woman *stole* the armor. Not a squeaky clean little heroine after all," Desaad murmured, staring into the video screen that displayed Diana's memory of how she had gotten the armor.

Of course, this is a very recent memory, Desaad thought. Diana had unexpected reserves of strength and it would take time to delve deeply into her past—to find out everything.

When the vivid dream-memory ceased, Desaad turned away, bored. He was, in fact, not interested in Diana herself, but only in what her dreams could tell him about Themyscira. And, of course, in any detail he could use to increase her suffering.

Most of Desaad's lab was crammed with esoteric

equipment whose main purpose was the creation of pain. He was a connoisseur, a master, who could cause agonies of exquisite subtlety or overwhelming power.

He secretly resented that his hand had been stayed against his Amazon prisoner. His more obvious methods would have already extracted the information his master required. But Desaad knew that data gained through torture could lack depth. And his master appreciated richness of detail.

Desaad shrugged. In time, knowledge would come. And another weapon would be placed in Darkseid's arsenal. But for now, Desaad would toy with her.

He would let Diana know that her memories themselves were betraying her island home, and that there was nothing she could do to stop them. Her helplessness would cut deep and bring an exquisite gush of psychic agony, thick and rich as her life's blood. And Desaad would drink deep.

He bowed his head in silent homage. Great Darkseid was right, as always. The fullness of time would meet his master's agenda—and Desaad's own.

The door to Diana's cell slid open and a hooded figure entered.

Diana stood, her interest quickening. Maybe now she could find out what was going on.

Desaad threw back his hood. "I have almost completed the analysis of your armor, Wonder Woman. If it proves practical, we will use it as a prototype to enhance the strength and agility of our Dog Soldiers. Your lasso is another interesting artifact—"

"It *won't* prove practical." Diana shrugged, apparently undisturbed. "The armor is powered by the goddess Athena and bonded to me alone. Only I can wield its power."

"I acknowledge that *you* believe that!" Desaad sneered. "But Themyscira is a particularly backward and unsophisticated little realm, with its marble temples and rustic glens. And that Temple of Athena, with its benevolent statue! Ah, well, you were brought up there, so what can one expect?"

Diana was shocked into silence.

Themyscira's sun-drenched beauty had dominated her thoughts and dreams. A temporary escape into its remembered loveliness had provided solace. But Desaad was talking about Themyscira as if he'd seen it—as if he'd been there. And that was impossible.

"Lord Darkseid will, of course, bring the place into

the present," Desaad continued. "He will rip the mineral deposits from its cliffs and build factories along its shores and—"

"He can't!" Diana cried.

"He is Darkseid," Desaad murmured. "He will do as he chooses with Themyscira, as he will with you."

"No!" Diana lunged forward, stretched her bonds to their limit, and kicked out with her foot. Desaad stepped nimbly backward and the blow narrowly missed his head.

A close call, he thought, *but taunting her is worth the danger.* He could feel Diana's anguish. He would see that it got worse.

"You stole the armor and relied on its magic to give you an edge in combat," Desaad continued. "Now Apokolips has stolen you. Once you are Bound to my master, Darkseid, I will return the armor to you, of course. And you will use it to carry out his will. Perhaps you will destroy the Justice League. Or Themyscira itself?"

Diana didn't yet understand, Desaad realized, but she would. Then she would fight him. It would take longer to force out her memories. But there would be greater pleasure in the victory.

Desaad bowed and left, but Diana hardly noticed, so engrossed was she in the puzzle of where Desaad had gotten his information.

I did take the armor, Diana thought. *I left Themyscira secretly, against my mother's will. But how could Desaad know that?* Funny, she'd just been half-asleep, vividly reliving the night she took her armor....

And then she understood. Her *dreams!* Somehow Desaad had been tapping into her dreams. In dreaming, by remembering, she had betrayed her beloved island and its people.

Even now, she felt memories welling up...felt herself beginning to sink into another reverie. But she fought against it as she had never fought before.

Why is this happening? Diana asked herself.

The guard shuffled in with an Energy Block and another pitcher of water. Suddenly Diana had her answer.

I'm being drugged, she thought. *There are drugs in that block of sawdust. Or in the water. Or both.*

Beyond her cell, down the corridor, she heard screams and moans. "Himon! Help us!" a voice cried.

They were Lowlies, the guard had told her. Fodder for Desaad's pleasure and Darkseid's designs.

But Himon, the legendary Himon, had escaped. Diana wished she knew how. Because she had to get out of here too. And soon.

CHAPTER
5

It was easy to disguise the fact that she wasn't eating, Diana thought as she crumbled the Energy Block into sawdust and scattered it over the grime-encrusted floor. Not much of a sacrifice either, considering the menu, even without the piquant addition of mind-altering drugs.

She trusted that, in the dim light, the guard wouldn't notice a bit more grime. Or the water she spilled between the cracks in the stone floor.

An old adage from her training days came back to her: "Hunger sharpens a warrior's wits." Well, this hunger was sure to. Of course, she would have to escape before she died of thirst.

From time to time she would notice that she had

slipped into a dream-state, would realize that she had vividly relived a fragment of a memory. Another piece for Desaad's Amazon collection.

Diana hoped that as her mind grew sharper she would be better able to resist.

By the second day, Diana was very thirsty. Despite her best efforts to consider the problem of the present, her fractious mind kept veering back into the past. . . .

THE HUNT

The sun beats down, but Diana ignores her thirst. She'll drink later, after she finds her quarry. This is more than a training session or one of her mother's endless tests.

The monster she stalks this time is real.

Since Diana's early childhood, her mother had been devising a gauntlet of trials, supposedly to honor Athena, Goddess of Wisdom and War, and to demonstrate Diana's warrior prowess. Diana had always resented the tests and, as she neared womanhood, had begun to insist that she be allowed to honor Athena in her own way.

For this Feast Day, Diana announced that she would hunt the enormous dragon that was decimating local flocks and had carried off a shepherdess.

"The gods protect Themyscira from outside danger. But there are still dangers inherent to this island," she had told her mother. "I need to use my skills to help our people!"

Diana spots the dragon on a high crag, where it is devouring its latest kill. Tossing aside her shield and spear, she notches an arrow in her bow, takes careful aim, and lets it fly.

The arrow strikes the dragon's chest. But instead of falling, the dragon sweeps high into the air, and its spreading wings seem to blot out the sun.

Diana fires arrow after arrow at the dragon as it dives at her, breathing fire and roaring so loudly the ground shakes. Its eyes glow red, lit by its internal fires, and its fangs are long and sharp as scimitars.

The dragon is almost upon her when she throws aside her bow. She grabs her shield and spear, and using the shield to deflect its fiery breath, she thrusts *the spear into its opened mouth and forces the point up into its brain.*

She rolls aside as the dragon's massive body crashes to the earth.

Diana stands over the magnificent fallen monster, whose scales gleam like gold. Its skin will make Athena an appropriate offering, she thinks.

Diana has used her abilities for the good of her people. Yet something is missing.

They didn't need *me* for this, *she realizes.* A hunting party could have slain the beast.

Then she sighs. Where is a challenge only I can face?

Oh well, *she thinks.* At least I'm free of testing for another year.

Diana blinked. . . . Another memory given to Desaad.

Enough! she told herself. *I've got to think!*

She saw again, in her mind's eye, her spear point stabbing upward. And she thought, *My energy bonds can be severed. Just like* that!

When the guard opened the door, he found Diana writhing on the floor, foam bubbling from her mouth.

"Good try!" he said. "Seen that one before. Get up, 'fore I report you to Desaad. He'll have you writhin' for real."

Still carrying the water pitcher and Energy Cube, the guard stepped closer and lashed out with his foot. Even as his toe connected, Diana jerked his legs out from under him and he found himself sprawled on the floor beside her.

Diana grabbed the dagger from his belt and slammed its hilt upward into the underside of his chin, knocking him unconscious. He jerked and lay still.

Diana sat up. "Something tells me you aren't used to prisoners fighting back," she told him. He had left the door slightly ajar when he entered. All she had to do now was reach it and escape.

She was hoping the knife would sever the wires of her energy shackles and free her. Of course, she might also electrocute herself. But that was a chance she would have to take.

She hacked at the thick wires. Yes, one was almost cut through. She pressed carefully with the point of the blade. There was a loud pop! A huge spark leapt from the wire and she was thrown back against the wall.

The light in the hall went out.

Diana struggled to her feet in the darkness. This was better than she had hoped. The shackles had fallen away. Her hands were free. And she had shorted out part of the building.

The good news was she would be able to make at least part of her escape under cover of darkness. The bad new was someone—probably a lot of someones—would very soon be rushing in this direction.

Shuffling toward the door, she nearly tripped over the guard. She hesitated, and considered taking his armor and helmet as a disguise.

As if that would work, she thought. *Better to travel light and keep out of sight.*

Tossing aside the half-melted dagger, she felt her way along the wall, out of her cell, and into the corridor. She pulled the cell door shut behind her.

She couldn't see a thing, had no idea where to go now.

Her wrist was starting to hurt where the shackle had sparked and burned, but she would worry about that later. If there was a later.

Somewhere ahead she heard a door open and saw a burly figure silhouetted against a rectangle of light that led to a stairwell.

The guard cursed hoarsely, but didn't sound alarmed.

"Old wiring," he grunted. "Told Desaad we'd need an upgrade." Then he shouted, "Kranx, Kranx, where are you, man?"

The cries of the prisoners, their sighs and sobs, curses and screams, almost drowned out Kranx's answer from inside Diana's dungeon cell.

"Help! Help me! I'm in here!"

CHAPTER
6

As the burly guard began to sweep the corridor with light from a hand-torch, Diana stepped forward, then leapt high into the air, taking him on the chin with the point of her heel.

He crashed to the floor like a toppled statue.

Diana pulled from his belt a cylindrical object that she thought was a weapon. She had never used a gun—they didn't have them on Themyscira—but she understood the principal. Point and fire. She would use it if she had to.

She sighed. Green Lantern would probably see her lack of practice with modern weapons as further proof she was an amateur. But she was a fast learner. And she would do whatever it took to get her armor back.

Diana stepped over the unconscious guard, into the rectangle of light. She stood on a narrow landing. To the right, stone steps climbed upward. To the left, they descended.

Up or down? she wondered. From the damp coolness, she assumed her cell was underground. But she had no idea how to find Desaad's lab.

She heard the tramp of feet on the stairs below. Probably more guards checking on the power outage. That settled it.

She dashed quietly upward.

From below, she heard someone shove open the door to the darkened corridor, heard his exclamation of dismay.

She doubled her speed, sprinting up past another landing, aware that it was just a matter of time before the alarm sounded. How far below ground was she now? How close to Desaad's Lab? How close to escape?

Then, from below came the dreaded wail of an alarm.

Even as she climbed past another landing, she could hear feet pounding up the stairs behind her, hear the rattle of armor. In mere seconds they would spot her.

The door she had just passed slammed open. She glanced backward and saw two officers rush onto the landing. The officers gaped at the tangle of guards rushing up the stairs right at them.

The guards pointed up at Diana, and the confused officers turned, openmouthed, to stare at her.

As they started to draw their weapons, Diana pivoted and leapt into the air, kicking out at one of the officers, hitting him in the chest. He toppled down the stairs and slammed into the upsurge of guards, hitting them like a cannonball. The men sprawled backward under the impact.

Diana spin-kicked the second officer, who plunged after his companion. She saw with satisfaction a writhing mass of guards tumbling down the steps like a rock slide of armored bodies, blocking the path of others on their way up.

So far so good, she thought.

Then she heard footsteps clambering down the stairwell from above.

A hoarse voice ordered her to surrender. An energy blast ripped past her head and ricocheted down the corridor, hitting the guards in the tumbled heap below, adding to the confusion.

That explained why no one had fired at her before.

Diana pointed her own weapon at the descending officer and pulled the trigger. The officer grabbed for the wall and doubled over, retching noisily.

"Disorientation . . . rod," he tried to shout up to those who followed him. "She has a—" He retched again, then toppled down the stairs and landed at her feet.

Nasty but nonlethal, Diana thought. *A useful weapon, indeed.* She crouched beside the officer.

"Desaad's Laboratory," she said. "Where is it?"

"Lab . . . ?" He looked confused. Then his eyes rolled back in his head and he fainted.

Diana couldn't go back down the staircase. That way was blocked. Nor could she go up. She would have to leave the stairwell and take her chances in the corridor beyond.

She ducked out the doorway into a carpeted hall hung with rich tapestries and elegantly furnished with gilded chairs and couches. Desaad, it seemed, lived well.

As she was bolting shut the stairwell door, a blast of energy seared her arm. She dove aside and other blasts bounced off the door and ricocheted around the hall, shattering fine statues and ripping glowing holes in elegant tapestries.

She swept the room with a disorientation blast. Two officers reeled forward and collapsed onto the carpet. But more guards would be coming.

At the end of the hallway, tall gothic windows with decorative panes of leaded glass revealed only darkness. It was impossible to see what lay beyond.

Should she try to fight her way through to Desaad's Lab—wherever that was—to retrieve her armor? Or retreat strategically and return for her armor when she actually had a plan?

Officers bristling with weapons surged into the hall. Their overwhelming numbers convinced her. She couldn't win against them all.

She fired the disorientation weapon, felling the first few who appeared. She snatched a thick cloak from one of the fallen and wrapped it around herself as she ran toward the window. She dove through it and fell amid a shower of shattered glass.

Diana landed atop a sticker bush—probably what passed for landscaping on Apokolips, she thought. Still wrapped in the protective cloak, she rolled off and away from the bushes and onto bare concrete.

She was covered with cuts and scratches from glass and thorns. But the bush had broken her fall. She was alive.

Energy ripped through her leg and peppered the ground. *They're shooting from the broken window,* she thought.

She pointed the disorientation rod up and fired. There was a momentary lull.

She was in a courtyard, surrounded by a high stone rampart. If she could scale it, she just might escape alive. But as she ran closer, she realized it was taller than it appeared, and cleverly constructed so that the upper edge far overhung the wall. She couldn't jump to the top and wouldn't be able to scale it after all.

She heard a menacing growl and the scrape of claws on concrete. She whirled. In near silence, huge mastiffs, as big as ponies, bore down on her. Their fangs slashed the darkness like glittering knives.

A terrifying sight, but one Diana welcomed.

In a flash of hyperintense memory, Diana realized that these demon dogs would be her salvation.

THE DANCE OF DEATH

Diana, nearly a woman now, insists on choosing her own demonstration to honor Athena. And her mother, happy that, for once, Diana seems cooperative, gives her approval.

Diana is beginning to hope that someday she and Hippolyta will be able to reach a truce in their battle of wills, based on mutual respect. But she is still young enough to want to annoy her mother—just a little.

The Amazons long ago imported the Minoan game of bull-dancing, in which an acrobat leaps upon the back of a charging bull, balances there for a stride or two, then cartwheels off onto the ground, only to do it all over again. It is dangerous and not to be engaged in lightly. Queen Hippolyta has made it clear she disapproves of the sport, which is reason enough for Diana to love it.

So, in the Arena, before all Themyscira, Diana honors Athena with a public demonstration of bull-dancing.

Later, with a mischievous grin, she tells her mother that, while bull-dancing is still a game like all Hippolyta's trials, at least it was a real test of her gymnastic prowess and a true contest of wills between herself and the bull.

So, when the mastiffs charged, Diana was ready. She vaulted past the lead dog's enormous jaws, landing upright on its back. The dog skidded to a halt, turning to snap at her. But it was too late.

Another powerful flip had already carried her to the top of the overhanging wall.

Then she was off the wall and crouching in a litter-filled alley, silently blessing her mother for the endless hours of gymnastics training she'd forced her daughter to endure. Today, that training had saved Diana's life.

Energy blasts pulsed over the wall. She heard officers shouting for tracker hounds and aerotroopers.

Leaping to her feet, Diana tucked the disorientation rod into the sash at her waist, and ran for her life.

CHAPTER
7

The alley ended against another, and Diana screeched to a halt. *Which way?* she wondered. *Left or right?* What did it matter, as long as it led away from Desaad!

Diana sprinted left, then right down another alley, and she emerged on a narrow, nearly deserted street lined with grimy shops and tenements. A few dark figures melted into the shadows as she sped past.

She ran without the slightest notion of where she was going. The light was dim but, somehow, all-pervasive. There were no consistent shadows to help her gauge direction. She hoped she wasn't traveling in circles.

What would Batman do? she wondered. That was easy. He'd reason his way out of the problem.

Diana craned her neck upward, desperately searching for landmarks. Behind her, a faceless edifice loomed like a massive tombstone, its top fading eerily into the sulfurous smog. Darkseid's citadel, she thought—the seat of all power on Apokolips.

She thought she recognized Desaad's dungeon-filled manor off to the right. At least she seemed to be heading toward safety.

The howl of hounds on a scent shook her and instinctively she leapt for the air. Nothing happened. She no longer had her armor.

Not for the first time, Diana regretted its loss. She wondered if depending on it had somehow crippled her, made her less able to survive on her own, without its mystical aid.

Get over it! she told herself. She couldn't fly, so she'd have to find another way to get the hounds off the scent.

The crumbling tenement buildings were separated by mean, mazelike passageways. If she could reach the rooftops, she could leap from roof to roof and lose them that way.

Diana ducked into the foyer of a particularly grim-looking building and darted up dilapidated stairs. Suspicious eyes peered through cracks. A door clicked shut as she dashed past.

On the top-floor landing, she climbed a rickety ladder, pushed aside a trapdoor, and clambered onto the roof. She heard the baying of the hounds in the foyer below, and a jumble of voices.

"Whoever she is, we ain't hiding her!"

"She ran up there!"

"So much for the poor and downtrodden sticking together," Diana muttered.

She could hear the hounds scrabbling eagerly up the stairs, and the shouts of their handlers as they followed.

Diana took a running start, leapt across an alley-wide space, and landed on the roof next door. She glanced back, expecting to hear the hounds howling their frustration at the bottom of the ladder.

But she had underestimated the abilities of the massive hounds. Someone had thrown open the trapdoor and a huge dog shape was emerging laboriously from the opening. On its back was a saddle, and in that saddle sat an armored soldier.

Trick dogs—part of a Dog Cavalry, she thought. *Somehow, it figures.*

She sprinted forward, made a desperate leap for the roof beyond. And the roof beyond that.

Two hounds were on the roof now. One was stopped by the gap between buildings, but the lead hound leapt it fearlessly and kept on coming. He also took the next with ease.

Diana raced ahead of him, desperate now to escape. And realized the next gap spanned no alley but an actual street. It was too wide to clear, even for her.

One more hurdle and the massive hound would be on the roof with her. She couldn't let herself be trapped there.

She glanced around, spotted the trapdoor. If she couldn't go over, she'd have to go down.

"Halt!" a voice from overhead shouted.

Aerotroopers dove out of the sky, drawn by the baying of the hounds. They looked like ski jumpers in their skintight, aerodynamic jumpsuits, balancing precisely on their flying aerodiscs.

They pointed weapons at Diana. "Give it up—or we feed you to the hound!"

Not a chance, she thought. *Not when I've come this far. If I had a weapon—*

Then she remembered the disorientation rod.

The hound was nearly upon her. She pointed the rod at it and fired. Then she swept it up at the aerotroopers.

Dog and rider collapsed in a heap, then began to struggle to their feet. The hound growled menacingly. Above her, the aerotroopers were wavering on their discs, but all were still upright.

"Your rod's out of juice!" one of them shouted. "Surrender! It's Darkseid's will!"

"Oh, *that* will convince me!" Diana muttered. She shouted, "You want me, come and get me!"

And suddenly, everything was happening at once.

Diana hurled the empty weapon at the lead trooper's head, dove, and rolled for the trapdoor, even as the aerotroopers opened fire. She flung open the trapdoor and had rolled halfway inside when the lead aerotrooper's body fell beside her.

The rod she had thrown must have connected and knocked him out cold, she thought. In a blinding flash, she realized she finally had what she had been wishing for. She had just been handed the Apokoliptian equivalent of wings.

She hauled the trooper through the opening,

dropped him down the ladder to the floor below, and bolted the trapdoor shut behind her.

Let them hammer at it, she thought.

Other troopers would probably come at her up the stairs, to catch her between them. She had maybe half a minute to figure out how the discs worked.

She pulled the discs from the trooper's feet. They came off reluctantly. Ah, now she saw. They were attached magnetically, through the soles of his boots.

She ripped off the trooper's boots and stuffed her own feet into them. The fit wasn't bad.

Then she stepped onto the discs.

Now what? she wondered. *How are they controlled?* When she had knocked the trooper unconscious, the discs had fallen with him, she reasoned. *So consciousness must control them. Volition. Will!*

Diana willed herself to rise. And did so, balancing carefully. *Excellent! Mother always said I was too strong-willed for my own good.* She almost laughed . . . until she heard the shouts of aerotroopers as they skimmed up the stairwell.

She couldn't go up or down. Luckily there was another way out.

Diana had been dimly aware of doors cracking open, of malevolent eyes peering out at her.

Now she flew forward, crashing with all her might into one of those doors. It flew open, sending the hovel's occupant sprawling backward onto the floor. On the opposite wall was an open window.

Diana zoomed through the hovel and, crouching low, soared outside.

Behind her, she could hear the man shouting, "That way, troopers! I couldn't stop her! She went out that way!"

Diana dropped straight down toward the street. At the second-floor level she rounded a corner and ducked agilely into an alley. She hovered in the shadows as dark shapes glided overhead.

Aerotroopers looking for her. *What now?* If she stayed here, she knew, eventually one of the downtrodden citizens of this slum would report her whereabouts.

Diana stared up at the dense smog that shrouded the upper level of the city. She would hide up there!

She floated silently roof-ward and glanced around. Several blocks away, flying figures were circling in the mist, searching the streets below. None seemed to be looking her way.

Better make it fast, she decided.

She could feel the G-force as she rode the aerodiscs upward. One glimpse of the city jumbled before her, then she was enveloped in hazy nothingness.

Within the smog-vapor she was flying blind. But if she couldn't see anything or anyone, then they couldn't see her either. She would have to rely on her other senses for information.

Below, she could hear the troopers' staccato shouts, punctuating a steady ominous background roar. *Traffic?* she wondered. *Or some as yet unknown danger?* Sounds echoed oddly in this smog. It was impossible to guess where they originated. Or what they might be.

In the distance, there was a whip-crack explosion. The all-pervasive smog flickered orange and the stench of sulfur became overpowering.

The more she experienced Apokolips, the more terrible it seemed. And yet, people were born here, lived here, and died here without the hope of anything better.

She was lost, bleeding, weaponless, but at least *she* was free. She was one of the lucky ones.

Soon, she would return to Desaad's palace and take back her armor.

But right now, Job One was staying alive.

CHAPTER

8

Diana slowly drifted into growing darkness as the surrounding haze deepened from pearl to gray to almost black. For the first time in days she had time to consider, and her thoughts disturbed her.

She had faced guards, a Dog Cavalry, and aerotroopers without her armor and had escaped with little more than flesh wounds. Either Darkseid's soldiers were inept (though that wasn't their reputation) or they were reluctant to kill her.

If so, why? What is really going on? she wondered.

Diana found her onslaught of memories equally disturbing. Probably the flashbacks were caused by the drugs she had been given, but she was experiencing them not as reminiscences now, but as realities that overlaid the world around her. What if, eventually, the past overwhelmed the present and she stood frozen, unable to function?

Her reverie was broken by a flare of orange brilliance and a deafening salvo, like fireworks. Heat and a sulfur stench hit her like a wall.

Her eyes streamed. She coughed raggedly.

She didn't fool herself that Desaad's minions had given up searching for her. But she must be miles from his palace, she reasoned. She willed herself to drop below the hideous clouds so she could take a look around.

Apokolips was a panorama of lights that stretched as far as the eye could see. In the distance, the source of the orange roar was an intermittent flickering amidst billowing vapor. What was it? she wondered. An erupting volcano? A chemical fire? A nuclear meltdown?

All seemed unlikely.

She dropped even lower, hovering above another run-down area. But this, at least, had some life to it.

Vehicles of all sizes and shapes, some wheeled, some gliding on force fields, inched through narrow streets thronged with people going about their business, apparently unconcerned by the orange roar on the horizon.

Whatever the explosions were, they must be business as usual on Apokolips.

Diana landed on a roof that faced a crossroads. She leaned over its parapet, studying the crowd, observing what they wore, how they talked.

She needed food and drink, and to wash away the blood and tend her wounds. Soon she would have to go below and pass as one of them.

She heard a scream and a thump from the alley beside her. Instantly she was in the air.

Below, a thug in a hooded tunic struck another man with a club. The victim screamed, waving a satchel that clinked with coins, trying to buy his way out of a beating. The thug grabbed the satchel, then brought down the club to finish his victim off.

Instinctively, Diana dropped out of the air and into the mugger, knocking him aside, unconscious.

The astounded victim scrabbled backward toward the street, pleading for his life, telling her to keep the money and just leave him alone. When he reached the sidewalk, the victim stumbled to his feet and was gone.

Diana picked up the abandoned satchel. It was heavy with coins. With it, she could buy food instead of stealing. But she couldn't join the crowd covered in rags and blood.

She eyed the unconscious robber's clothing speculatively. She had noticed that men and women alike wore trousers and tunics, military-looking jumpsuits, or even armor. The mugger's clothing was a motley mixture of leather and mail, probably random pieces stolen from his victims.

Superman and the others would probably disapprove of this, Diana thought. But here on Apokolips, the law of the jungle prevailed. She'd have to adapt if she wanted to survive.

So she began to strip the mugger and assemble her disguise.

Diana emerged from the alley, wearing a hooded leather tunic with a red design on the shoulder and mail breeches that fit her like a second skin. They were tight, but they covered her incriminating wounds.

She wore the aerotrooper boots but had left the discs hidden beneath her bloody, torn rags in the alley. They were too large to hide in the satchel, and since they were military issue, she dared not be seen with them.

Moving with the crowd, she caught her reflection in a gritty window. If she could wash the grime off, she thought, she would be fairly presentable. At least for Apokolips.

Diana nearly trampled the man ahead of her when he stopped abruptly, gaping skyward.

Flying low, scanning the crowd, came a wedge of Parademons. The people around her broke into excited whispers.

"Parademon patrol!"

"Who're they hunting?"

"Escaped prisoner!"

Diana ducked her head—surely they wouldn't notice one more bowed head among so many others—and slipped into the next open doorway.

Diana found herself in an Apokoliptian diner.

She studied the dimly lit room casually. It was crisscrossed with exposed beams. Pipes snaked haphazardly up walls and across the rafters. Weapons, medals, and pictures of dashing female warriors adorned the walls. Above the counter, in a place of honor, hung a portrait of Darkseid, Ruler of Apokolips.

Tables crowded the sawdust-strewn floor, and at them, powerful-looking women in clothing ranging from crisply military to skimpily casual sat drinking, eating, gaming, and laughing noisily. Some were armed.

Delicious smells wafted from the kitchen.

Copying the other patrons, Diana shoved her way to the counter, ordered food and drink, and fumbled with the unfamiliar money. She plonked down a large coin and told the server to keep the change. He grinned happily.

She grabbed her order, elbowed her way to an empty table in a rear corner, and began to eat, drink, and eavesdrop.

The patrons were what they looked like, Diana realized—elite soldiers, representatives of a culture of war, an Apokoliptian version of the Amazons. For the first time in days, Diana began to relax, feeling comfortable among such a sisterhood. *Their loyalty will be to other women,* she thought.

But when she glanced at the portrait of Darkseid, she wasn't so sure.

A blond giantess with a broad, cheerful face bumped Diana's table as she shoved past carrying full mugs. Diana's drink slopped onto the tabletop.

"Sorry," the blonde said.

Diana shrugged. "No problem."

Blondie moved past. Her red-haired friend followed, carrying several bowls of stew.

Red-Hair stopped before Diana, squinting at her suspiciously. "You're from the Seventeenth." She sneered toward the insignia on Diana's tunic. "What're you doing *here*?"

Diana groaned. She must be wearing the emblem of a rival division. Just her luck! Uncertain how to answer, Diana bluffed, "Special assignment. Who wants to know?"

"Blood Red of the Female Furies," Red answered. "What *special* assignment *was* that, soldier?" She looked around, making sure the others were watching her roust this interloper. "Same kind that got the entire Seventeenth transferred to Night-Time, after the fracas at the Slum Section 8 Vehicle Dump?"

Diana had no idea what Blood Red was talking about, but she answered coolly, "What I'm doing here is none of your business."

"That so?" sneered Red. "I say you're AWOL! What's your name and rank? Who's your commanding officer?"

"That's not your business either," Diana sneered.

"I'm making it my business," growled Red.

Three things were clear, Diana thought. Red was spoiling for a fight. They were drawing unwanted attention. And the questions were beyond her ability to answer.

The Flash would think of a clever comeback, Diana thought. *But wit would probably be lost on Red, anyway.*

So Diana fell back on tradition. She overturned her table, spattering Red and the patrons behind her with the remnants of her dinner, toppling Red and the stew she carried onto Blondie, who careened onto a nearby table in an almost comical domino effect.

"You and what army?" Diana asked.

CHAPTER

9

In a single fluid motion, Red pushed herself upright and leapt, panther-like, for Diana.

Diana sidestepped, grabbed Red by the scruff of her neck, and tossed her headfirst into an adjacent table. Red slammed facedown in the middle of a dicing game, sending stacks of coins rattling onto the floor.

"Get off!" growled a braided Valkyrie, roughly shoving Red onto the floor. "Darkseid's teeth, woman, I was winning!"

"Find your coins if they mean that much to you!" Red snarled, pulling the woman onto the floor, slamming into yet another table that overturned noisily.

The diner erupted joyfully in a maelstrom of fists

and feet. The owner sank behind the counter, groaning, "Not again!"

Diana sidled toward the door, hoping the crowd would be so distracted and entertained by the brawl that she could slip quietly away.

But Blondie grabbed Diana's shoulder. "You mess with Red, you mess with me!" she said.

Diana froze. Blondie had grabbed her energy-scored shoulder, and the pain was almost blinding. But it was memory that immobilized Diana. . . .

GANG FIGHT

It makes no sense.

Diana knows that, even as she trips one attacking Amazon, parries the sword-thrust of another with her right hand, and kicks the blade from the hand of a third. Diana's left hand snatches up the falling blade before it hits the ground.

Nine attackers are down and disarmed now, three more to go. One of those three Diana faces, swords to sword. Two are behind her.

With a quick riposte, Diana disarms her opponent. A kick sends the attacker sprawling.

As Diana expects, the two behind rush at her. She sprints toward a wall with her attackers in hot pursuit, believing Diana plans to face them with the wall guarding her back.

But Diana doesn't do the expected. She leaps up the wall, flips backward over the heads of her opponents, and lands behind them.

She presses the points of the two swords she holds into their backs.

"You're out of the fight!" she says.

Diana is victorious. Twelve warriors beaten in a single melee and she is still an adolescent.

The arena erupts in applause and Hippolyta beams proudly from her carved wooden throne.

The real battle comes later.

"What does it matter, Mother, if I win or lose?" Diana rages as she paces her mother's chamber. "Training for combat, fighting mock battles! How can these things honor Athena when there's no wisdom in it?"

"That's nonsense, Diana," Hippolyta says. "We Amazons are warriors. You are my heir and will someday be Themyscira's queen!"

Diana rolls her eyes. "Mother, you're an immortal. I won't ever be queen! Why do we even need warriors? The gods protect Themyscira. We are at peace, have always been at peace, will always be at peace!"

"Someday, a champion may be needed," Hippolyta says firmly. "And, if that day comes, Diana, wisdom suggests that you be ready!"

In some amazement, Diana realized that, while her mind was in the past, her body was reacting automatically in the present.

She had grabbed Blondie's wrist and flipped her against yet another table, kicked another Fury backward, and tripped up a third.

Even now, someone was swinging a chair at Diana's head.

But Diana spun sideways to avoid it and kicked out at the swinger, knocking her backward into another group of fighters, who went down under the impact.

Someone grabbed at Diana's hood, and her dark hair tumbled free. Diana sent the woman sprawling.

The bodies piled up around Diana as she continued her dance of bloodless violence. This *was* her art, she realized. What she was good at. What she loved. How had her mother *known*?

Then Red staggered to her feet, clutching a dagger long as a sword.

"Don't!" Blondie yelled. "Red, no! Fun's fun, but bloodshed's against orders!"

But Red, in the grip of a mindless fury, rushed at Diana, murder in her eye.

Diana kicked Red's feet out from under her, twisted the knife from her hand, and slammed Red backward onto the floor. Diana knelt over her attacker, Red's own knife pointed at the woman's throat.

The other Amazons grew silent.

"Go on," Red snarled. "I drew on you! It's your right! No one could blame you—"

"My right?" Diana said.

Blondie looked disgusted. "You know—to kill her!" she said.

For a moment, Diana held the point to Red's throat. Then she threw the knife aside and got to her feet. "Why waste a good warrior?" she asked.

"She's right," the Valkyrie intoned solemnly. "We belong not to ourselves, but to Darkseid."

"Hail, Darkseid!" they all chanted in unison.

Diana almost rolled her eyes. How had Darkseid managed to brainwash an entire world? But at least, finally, she had said the right thing.

Blondie pulled Red to her feet.

The Furies all seemed in fine spirits now, righting the tables and chairs, calling for more food and drink.

Red brushed herself off, eyeing Diana curiously. "Unusual fighting style," she said. "None of us could touch you!"

"Higher-ups got you slated for a crack at the Special Powers Force, don't they?" said Blondie. "*That's* your special assignment, right?"

"Gotta be!" said the Valkyrie. "If she was with the Seventeenth, she was the *only* decent fighter they had!"

Another group of Furies crowded into the restaurant, excitedly discussing the Parademon patrols and the rumored escape of one of Desaad's prisoners.

Diana subtly led the discussion to Desaad, hoping someone would know the location of his lab within his manor. She was so engrossed in the conversation that she hardly noticed when Red's gaze rested on her speculatively. Or when Red excused herself and temporarily disappeared into the crowd.

CHAPTER
10

"What are you thinking, you young oafs, inviting a stranger into your midst?" said a cold, high voice behind them.

The talking, laughing Furies fell silent.

As one, they turned to face a bony woman with a head too large for her spindly body. Her short dark hair was slicked back from her high widow's peak and shaped into affected spit curls that framed her face. Her eyes were flat, like a snake's, and the color of poison. She wore not armor, but a long-sleeved tunic, and carried a multi-pronged harpoon-like blade.

She may have looked unimpressive compared to the robust, armored giantesses who surrounded Diana, but the younger Furies were plainly in awe of her.

Red stepped forward, dragging Diana to face the newcomer. "Bernadeth, this is the warrior I told you about."

Red told her about me? Diana wondered. *When? Why?* She began to feel a trickle of alarm.

Red looked at Diana smugly. "Bernadeth will be able to answer all your questions about the Lord Desaad. Because, you see, she is his sister."

His sister! Diana thought, dismayed. *Great Hera, can it get any worse?*

"You've been betrayed, of course—Wonder Woman!" Bernadeth said. Diana's horrified expression obviously amused her. "Red always was a resentful loser. But she *is* clever. She alone realized your true identity."

The other Furies looked confused. Bernadeth glanced at them contemptuously. "That, you idiots, is my brother's runaway. Desaad will arrive soon to collect her."

"Then Desaad will have made the trip for nothing," Diana snarled.

She snatched up a metal staff that was lying across a chair, swung it around her head, then smashed it across a tabletop. The table collapsed into splinters.

The Furies trained their weapons on Diana, but Bernadeth signaled them to step back.

"She single-handedly defeated all of you—as well as a number of my brother's minions," Bernadeth said. "But she will find *me* a more challenging opponent."

THE DUEL

Enough is enough!

Diana holds a gleaming sword, but refuses to raise it.

For this Feast Day, Hippolyta ordered a test of Diana's swordsmanship against her teacher, Xanthe. Diana argued that it was stupid to test her when everyone already knew she was the most skilled swordswoman on Themyscira. But Hippolyta insisted. At her command, Diana was garbed in her finest chiton and led to the arena.

Diana glances over at Xanthe, then scowls up at her mother, who watches from her throne, surrounded by Amazons eager for spectacle.

She can drag me here, *Diana thinks,* but she can't make me perform like a trained monkey, just so she can brag about what a great warrior I am.

Hippolyta calls out, "Begin!"

Xanthe, sword in hand, salutes Hippolyta, then Diana. Diana just stands there.

She begins to circle Diana cautiously, as if looking for an opening. Diana gazes ahead mulishly.

Her teacher lunges at Diana. Diana refuses to parry. She refuses to move at all.

The older Amazon glances uncertainly toward Hippolyta, asking wordlessly, "What do I do now?"

Diana raises an eyebrow at Hippolyta tauntingly, relishing her mother's embarrassed, frustrated glare.

Then Hippolyta's jaw juts out, mirroring Diana's own mulish expression. "Continue, Xanthe!" Hippolyta says. "If my daughter chooses not to defend herself, so be it!"

Xanthe lunges at Diana, her sword slashing.

Diana glances down, and her eyes widen with shock as blood wells thick and red from a cut on her sword arm.

Diana glares accusingly at her mother. But Hippolyta sits unmoved, arms folded.

Xanthe slashes again. Another cut drips red.

Diana begins to get angry. How can her own mother

let this happen? How can she calmly watch Diana's lifeblood drip onto the sand?

Another prick. And another. Fury rises like a geyser in Diana's breast—not at Xanthe, whose cuts are, in truth, little more than scratches—but at Hippolyta, who is trying to compel her obedience.

Diana whirls on Xanthe, shouts angrily, "Xanthe! Stop it! Now!"

But Xanthe slashes again, and finally Diana meets Xanthe's leaping blade with her own. With powerful, angry strokes, she forces Xanthe back toward her mother's dais. And knocks the blade from Xanthe's hand.

The Amazons are on their feet, cheering.

Diana raises her sword and snarls, "You command swordplay, Mother. So be it!"

With all her might, Diana flings the sword past Xanthe's head and sends it, quivering, into the backrest of her mother's wooden throne.

Diana sees Hippolyta's stunned expression and realizes what she has done. Her mother's betrayal infuriated Diana, but her own violent reaction has horrified her.

Diana bursts into tears.

Leaping the arena gate, she flees into the country-side, as if pursued by the demons of Hades.

As Diana stood frozen beneath the onslaught of memories, Bernadeth, quick and ruthless as the snake she resembled, struck with her pronged blade.

Diana, roused by the movement, jerked backward, and the tip of Bernadeth's blade slashed her leather tunic.

The Furies were shouting, wagering on who would win and how long the fight would last. It was like the arena all over again. Except this fight was real.

When Bernadeth thrust again, Diana caught one of the blade-prongs with the staff, jerked and twisted, trying to wrench the blade from Bernadeth's hand. But with surprising strength, Bernadeth yanked her pronged blade upward, slicing the metal staff in two.

That's no ordinary sword, Diana realized. It was sharper by far than it appeared. And Bernadeth was stronger and more dangerous than she looked.

No wonder the memory struck with such power, Diana thought. *I resented fighting Xanthe because my mother tried to force me. Bernadeth, too, is forcing this fight on me, but now I resent the time it is taking. Every second of delay brings Desaad closer. I have to find a way to end this quickly!*

Diana tossed the severed staff aside and leapt upward, grabbed an overhead pipe, and swung acrobatically atop a rafter.

Bernadeth, furious, slashed up at Diana, slicing through both rafter and pipe. Oil spurted from the pipe, spattering Bernadeth and fouling the room. The rafter sagged ominously.

Diana leapt gracefully for the next rafter and the next. Then she sprang down onto the floor and dashed toward the exit.

Howling with frustration, slipping on the oil-slicked floor, Bernadeth hurled her blade at Diana. Diana jerked backward, and the blade skewered the restaurant door. *Now I know how my mother felt when my own sword quivered so close to her head,* Diana thought.

She hauled open the door, dove outside, and tore around the corner of the building into the adjoining alley.

In the distance, she had glimpsed a wing of Parademons and, in their midst, a flying craft that, no doubt, held Desaad.

CHAPTER
11

Diana could hear Desaad's craft arriving in front of the restaurant. Bernadeth, in a foul temper, was cursing coldly as she tried to wrench her blade from the mutilated door. In seconds, Furies and Parademons would be pouring through streets and alleys, searching for her.

Diana looked around for a hiding place. The only possibility was a garbage transport that was trundling past the back end of the alley.

Not the preferred conveyance for a Princess of Themyscira, she thought wryly. But she dashed for the transport and, as it passed, grabbed hold of the back and climbed up into the open container.

The smell assaulted her. Taking shallow breaths,

she squelched through reeking refuse toward the back and crouched low, pulling a large, half-collapsed box up over her.

Just in time, she thought, as a wing of Parademons flew overhead. The only good thing about her present predicament was that the transport's very vileness would make it seem an unlikely escape vehicle.

But minutes later, to her horror, the transport lurched to a stop.

"Where're you headed?" Diana heard Blood Red's voice ask.

Just my luck, Diana thought. *Bernadeth assigned Red to help hunt me down.*

The hoarse voice of the driver answered, "Where I always head—out of Long-Shadow, through Armagetto, to the refuse dump in Night-Time. Why? What's up?"

"Escaped prisoner," Red said. "I'll have to search your transport."

The driver snorted. "Be my guest!"

Diana sank deeper beneath the mounds of nauseating refuse, thinking enviously of Martian Manhunter's ability to become insubstantial. She could use that power right now.

Red clambered onto the truck and poked the garbage randomly with her sword. Then she jumped down, muttering, "It will take me a week to disinfect my weapon!"

Serves you right! Diana thought.

She heard Red shout, "You're free to go!" And the transport lumbered on.

Diana thought wistfully of the aerodiscs hidden in a nearby alley, but with half of Apokolips actively searching for her, she didn't dare jump down to retrieve them.

She sighed. Every move she made to escape Desaad also took her farther from her armor.

Absently she pulled a fruit core from her hair. She wished she had thought to pull up her hood before diving into that muck.

She wondered if her hair would ever come clean.

She wished . . .

THE CHALLENGE

Diana treads water in a peaceful, spring-fed pool shaded by willows.

The coolness soothes her cuts, which she knows are

superficial and will heal without scarring. Despite her own willfulness, Xanthe had been careful not to really hurt her. But the quiet does little to calm her rebellious soul.

"What torments me is my own mother's cruelty!" Diana says aloud. "How could she have humiliated me like that?"

"I am also your queen," her mother says. "You know I could not let a public challenge to my authority go unanswered. Even from my own daughter."

Diana squelches that part of herself that knows Hippolyta is right. She faces her mother, says reproachfully, "I thought you loved me!"

Hippolyta sits on the bank. "You know I do. You are my moon and stars," she says. "Only your pride is truly hurt, Diana."

"But Xanthe is no match for me," Diana says. "And that was no true test. It was a performance, like a play with a ritual ending! It wasn't . . . real!"

"What is real is that you honor Athena and obey my orders. And that our people see your battle-prowess, and feel confident we can protect our home."

"From what? Nothing threatens us!" Diana argues. "My battle skills make me more dangerous than any

imaginary invader!" Her voice sinks to a whisper. "Look what I might have done to you!"

Hippolyta says, "My darling, had you meant it to, that sword would have pierced my heart. Despite your anger, you put it where you chose—because your training gave you the skill to do so!"

"But—" Diana begins to argue.

Hippolyta sighs. "Enough arguing, child. You meant to defy me, not kill me. You will now return with me to the arena, where you will publicly beg my pardon— and the pardon of Athena—for your insolence! And, in the future, you will exercise greater self-control."

Diana believes she herself was right. But she also knows her own behavior was inexcusable. The older she gets, the more tangled right and wrong seem to become!

She climbs sulkily from the pond. Though she hates being compelled to do anything, she will apologize for her behavior—she will even try to do so with good grace—though she would rather fight a hundred warriors. . . .

The jostling of the transport jerked Diana back to consciousness. She realized she had been dreaming. Great Hera, she felt tired enough to sleep, even wedged into a cesspit.

But it wasn't an ordinary dream, she realized. She had been mired in that memory. The flashbacks were getting more vivid. More real.

What was wrong with her?

Her eyes drifted shut. And this time, she slept undisturbed.

Diana was jolted awake by an explosive roar that rattled the transport like dice in a gambler's fist.

A flickering light shone fire-bright on the refuse, and the sulfur fumes had grown so strong they masked even the stench of the garbage.

Diana pushed the sheltering box aside, squelched to the back of the transport, and peered over the edge.

The transport was lumbering through a run-down industrial area riddled with scabrous-looking slums. Along one wall, in lettering five stories high, was the word ARMAGETTO. The dancing, dangerous light threw heat, sound, and eerie moving shadows over every surface.

The streets were so grim and all-pervasively hopeless that Hades itself was doubtless a cheerier place. The ragged inhabitants were covered in grime. Diana saw few guards or soldiers.

Now's my chance! she realized. *Dressed in a slashed tunic and covered in filth, I'll still seem well-dressed among those wretches.*

She glanced around, then climbed stiffly out of the transport and lowered herself onto the street.

She turned then and beheld the source of the appalling brightness—one of the vast and terrible planetary Fire Pits of Apokolips.

From a massive crater many miles across, an incandescent geyser gushed and churned, then rose high into the sky until it towered above the buildings of Armagetto. Then the blaze fell, fountain-like, into a pool of magma, only to rise again in flame and fury.

The Pit was rimmed by mines and power plants that converted the geothermal forces into energy to power Apokolips.

Beyond the buildings, Diana noticed small figures

laboring on a spar that jutted into that terrible con-
flagration. And, when the surface of the lava bubbled
and burst in volatile gouts of vapor, she saw those
people engulfed in flame and heard their high-
pitched screams.

CHAPTER

12

Diana raced forward, determined to help the casualties. But when she reached the edge of the Fire Pit, she saw that where people had stood, nothing—not even ashes—remained.

She had never imagined flames so all-consuming.

Then, from the shadow of one of the buildings, a foreman cracked a whip. To her consternation, more ragged workers—men, women, and yes! children—shuffled forward, zombie-like, to take the places of the slain.

Carrying sheets of metal, they filed onto a broad, horizontal pipe that jutted, pierlike, into that lake of fire. Steam was hissing from a long crack in the pipe, and apparently, the workers were enduring that unbearable heat and risking their lives to patch the hole.

Lava hissed and spattered, blistering their legs, but the workers moved forward, oblivious to the pain. One by one each worker laid his sheet of metal over the tear in the pipe, while another hammered it into place. Then each worker filed back to shore, retrieved another sheet of metal, and repeated the process.

Until the next *explosion comes,* Diana thought. *And all of* them *will also be destroyed.*

Then a child, maybe six or seven, stepped onto the pipe with his metal patch. He stumbled, then swayed. No one put out an arm to steady him or paid him any heed.

Diana could see the boy slipping, knew he was going to fall.

Diana leapt onto the pipe, glad of her thick-soled aerotrooper boots, and snatched the boy up before he toppled into the lava. She carried him to shore with a sinking feeling that she had just proclaimed her presence in Armagetto.

The foreman bellowed, "Hey, you! Stop!" Then he howled to his workers, "It's the escapee! Stop her, you Brain Bound Lowlies! Now!"

The Lowlies swept toward Diana like a wave.

She looked into their eyes and saw—nothing. Their faces were blank, expressionless, masklike. But their bodies reacted to the foreman's orders with blind obedience.

Still clutching the child to her, Diana turned and ran.

THE RESCUE

Diana shades her eyes and runs her square-sailed boat closer toward the fearsome whirlpools and eddies that mark the mystical barrier between Themyscira and the forbidden World of Men.

She has slipped away from the endless practicing for yet another Feast Day test. This time it was archery and javelins. Easy. Boring. Pointless.

Diana squints as sunlight strikes diamond glints from undulating waves. Again she spots that flash of white.

What is it? *she wonders.* A sounding dolphin? A piece of debris?

No, *Diana realizes.* Those are arms clinging to a

broken spar. And silver hair. A human of Man's World—being swept ever closer to the maelstrom barrier.

Then a swirling wave sweeps over the man and he disappears.

Amazon law tells Diana that Man is not allowed here. He must keep to his side of the barrier as she must stay on hers. There can be no contact between them.

But her heart says she cannot let him die.

Diana steers her boat toward the barrier. There is a slight resistance. Then she is through it, her boat plunging into the maelstrom after him.

When the silver head bobs to the surface, Diana is ready. Her preadolescent body dives through the water like a dolphin. And as the man sinks, she grabs his hair, hauling him back toward her boat.

What now? *she wonders.* I can't take him to Themyscira. No man can set foot there.

She drags him, gasping, into the bottom of her boat.

"Fishing boat sank," he croaks. "Drifted. Knew I was going to die. Thank you . . . young mermaid . . . for saving me. When you came . . . never saw anyone so beautiful . . . didn't think . . . you were real." *The man's eyes close and he rests.*

Diana studies his sagging belly, his stringy limbs with their knobby knees and wrists. Around his neck is a golden chain with an ancient coin pendant. His face is creased, like a wadded chiton left to dry in the sun.

He is old, Diana realizes with amazement. She has been taught that, unlike the Amazons of Themyscira, who live for centuries and never age, the lives of humans pass in the blink of an eye. Now she sees what that means and her heart is gripped by a terrible understanding.

Soon death will take this man, *she thinks*, but not today. Today, because of me, he is alive.

Defying the prohibitions of her people, Diana carries the man away from the barrier and toward the fishing lanes of the humans, where he will find others of his kind.

Soon they spot a boat and the old man stands and waves and shouts.

"My son," he tells Diana proudly. "He must've been out looking for me."

The old man sees that as the fishing boat tacks toward them, Diana is becoming worried. He takes the gold chain from around his neck and hands it to her. "A small treasure, young mermaid, for you to remember me by. Go now. I can make my own way from here!"

He dives into the sea and swims toward the fishing vessel.

And Diana sails back toward Themyscira, pondering the gulf between the law of her people and the ruling of her heart.

The chain with its ancient coin she leaves as a special offering for Athena. Her adventure she keeps hidden, though it gives her much to think about.

She has taken a secret step into Man's World and found it unlike anything she had been told. And she has used her superior strength and skill to save a helpless man who was unable to save himself.

For a while, at least, it makes her feel lucky and filled with important purpose. And her endless round of lessons becomes almost bearable.

The Fire Pit roared again its terrible roar. The child struggled in her arms, focusing her attention back to the present. While she had stood mesmerized, the Brain Bound had almost reached them.

Diana dashed past the power plants and into the slum beyond. Feet pounded behind her.

As she ducked into an alley, out of sight of her pursuers, the boy struggling in her arms cried out, "She's over here!"

"Hush," she tried to tell him. "You're safe with me!" But the boy looked at her with vacant eyes and kept on shouting.

The Brain Bound roiled down the alley, a flash flood of inhumanity. Diana sprinted into a courtyard, through another alley, and onto a narrow street beyond.

And all the while, the boy shouted, giving away her location.

Then, to her horror, she saw more Brain Bound up ahead. She turned. Others were behind her. She was trapped between them.

The Brain Bound howled their fury. And a screeching clamor answered from above.

Parademons dove from the sky, their weapons crackling with energy. A blast struck Diana's arm. Another ripped her side. She tried to shelter the boy with her body.

Then a blast struck her in the back and the boy broke free as she collapsed beneath a jumble of bodies and weapons, claws, and fists.

I could use Hawkgirl now, Diana thought. *To fly in and lift me into the air . . .*

But the hand that gripped her arm dragged her, instead, beneath the earth.

CHAPTER
13

Diana sank past concrete and rock and through a ceiling. A white-haired man was looking up as he pulled her into a dimly lit corridor.

He caught her body as it fell and laid her gently on a ledge. The pain in her back and shoulder and leg was receding now. She could no longer feel her arms or legs. Couldn't breathe . . .

DROWNING

. . . her lungs are burning, but she knows she cannot take a breath. She will need to swim farther down, to where the water begins to cool, in order to reach the

giant oyster and claim her prize. From the shape of its shell, Diana knows that within it lies a pearl as large as a hen's egg. Two more strokes and it will be hers.

Diana clutches the oyster, starts to lift it, to drag it to the surface, and is dismayed by its weight. She'll have to remove the pearl down here.

She draws her knife from the sheath at her waist, forces open the shell, and takes the glowing pearl. She kicks toward the surface. But she has taken too long, and she is too far under.

Her lungs are screaming— Breathe! Darkness begins to envelop her. And in the end, she sucks in water.

Then a wave of water buffets Diana, a strong hand grabs her chiton, dragging her upward. Her head breaks the water. Air strikes her face but can't inflate her flooded lungs. She is choking, dying.

She feels herself thrown onto the shore. Feels her back pressed. Hears her mother's voice command, "Breathe, Diana! Breathe!"

Water gushes out of her mouth. She coughs and sputters, and finally, she obeys. . . .

Diana breathed. *Mother,* she thought. *I'm all right.*

Only she wasn't. She was aware of pain from scores of wounds. She groaned and opened her eyes.

The man with the startling white hair was holding a silver fist-sized box above her body. The box made a pinging sound. And her many pains began to ease.

"Welcome back," he said. "I was afraid we'd lost you."

"Who . . . ?" she croaked.

"My name is Himon," he told her. "That blast ripped a hole in your lungs and nearly severed your spinal cord!" He saw her look of alarm.

"Don't worry," he continued. "Mother Box has patched up the worst of your wounds. But time's running short. They'll figure out what I've done and come into the tunnels after us. Can you walk now?"

Diana sat. Then stood. She hurt all over, and her legs wobbled, but they seemed to work.

Himon lifted his lantern. "Come! We're going into the deep tunnels where I have a safe area. Once we're there, Mother Box will finish healing you!"

On stiff and trembling legs, Diana followed him down an incline. "Himon, did you really pull me through the ceiling? How—?"

"Mother Box was tracking you for me," Himon told her. "When you collapsed, I phased up through the ground and grabbed you. You can thank Mother Box you're still alive."

Sounds came from the tunnel behind them. "The Brain Bound are in the tunnels. We must hurry."

Diana felt her mind whirling with new terms and concepts. Mother Box. Phasing. Brain Bound. Lowlies. It was hard to know what question to ask first.

"Brain Bound Lowlies— That's what their foreman called them! I thought Brain Bound was a kind of curse."

"In a way it is—but the curse is real," Himon said. "The ordinary citizens of Armagetto are called Lowlies. But your attackers weren't ordinary. Normal Lowlies couldn't withstand the heat of the Fire Pits. But the Brain Bound will work at whatever task they're given until their skin blisters off—until they die."

"And other Brain Bound take their places," Diana murmured.

Brain Bound, she thought. Wasn't that what Desaad had had in store for her?

LOST

Diana, soaked and gasping, struggles to sit up. "It's okay, Mother," she croaks. "I'm . . . okay!"

Hippolyta, dripping wet, her face white with shock, shakes Diana roughly. "You know you are never to dive alone, Diana! What can you have been thinking? Dearest Hera, if I had not realized you were missing . . . gone looking for you . . . I could have lost you!"

"Getting . . . offering . . . Athena's feast," Diana gasps.

But when she opens her hands, the pearl is gone. When she blacked out, it must have slipped through her fingers.

Himon shook Diana roughly.

"Snap out of it," he said. "Are you all right?"

"What?" Diana snapped into awareness. Himon was staring down the corridor, mindful of the ringing footsteps and clamor of voices.

She raised her hand to her forehead, trying to re-orient, to regain control before the memories overwhelmed her.

"I'm okay," she told him.

"Hurry, then!" Himon took her wrist. "This way! We're almost there."

Behind them, Parademons and Brain Bound jostled and grunted as they surged down a corridor.

She heard a Parademon shout, "There! She's—"

A blast of energy whizzed past Diana's head.

Then Himon was dragging her into a thick rock wall and out the other side.

Himon's hideout was furnished with a roughly made table, several chairs, and a sleeping pallet on the rocky floor. There was no door.

"This room was once a bubble in the lava," Himon said. He pulled bread and a hunk of cheese from a box and poured water into clay goblets. "I've made it habitable."

"All the comforts of home!" Diana sighed as she sank into a chair.

"What happened to you back there?" Himon asked.

Diana hesitated. How could she explain the overwhelming assault of memories? To buy herself time, she asked a question of her own.

"Why were you tracking me? Why did you and your . . . Mother Box . . . rescue me?"

"You tried to save the boy. For that alone I would have saved you, even if I hadn't realized you were Desaad's famous escapee," Himon said warmly. "That action marked you clearly as someone who didn't belong in Armagetto."

BELONGING

". . . you belong to Themyscira, Diana. And to me," Hippolyta says. "Don't you know, my moon and stars, that you're worth far more than any pearl?"

"Maybe," Diana tells her. "But I still think Athena would like the pearl. Better than watching me do gymnastics, anyway. I wish I hadn't dropped it. Now I'll never be able to find it."

Hippolyta shook Diana a little. "I forbid you to try, Diana. Do you understand?" Then she hugged her. "Sometimes you frighten me so! You're almost out of childhood now! Why must you always dash headlong into danger? Why can't you ever simply do as you're told?"

"I ... don't know. Truly, Mother," Diana whispers. "But something inside me needs to see and do and understand. ..."

"What?" Diana was startled. "Himon, did you say something?"

Himon looked at her with concern. "That's the third time you've sunk into a trance. Who are you exactly? And why did Desaad have you in his prison? What is going on?"

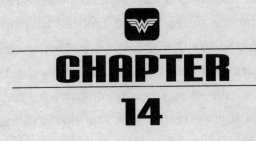

CHAPTER
14

Since her arrival on Apokolips, Diana had been imprisoned, chased, shot, battered, betrayed, and buried in garbage. At times, it had seemed the whole planet was against her. But Himon had saved her. He probably had his own agenda, but then, who on Apokolips didn't?

So Diana told him who she was and how she had been captured. How Desaad had stolen her armor, drugged her, and threatened her with Brain Binding. How the danger posed by Apokolips jeopardized Themyscira and all her Earth.

Himon questioned Diana closely about the increasing frequency and vividness of her flashbacks. Diana could see her answers disturbed him.

She had told herself the flashbacks were residual effects from the drugs Desaad had fed her. But she realized that at first her memories of Themyscira had seemed normal. Then, they had begun to overlay reality, like double images on photographs. Now, they had almost *become* reality. She was slowly losing herself in them.

Himon handed her a slice of bread. "Eat first. Then we'll ask Mother Box to examine you!"

Diana lay on her pallet while Himon held the cube he called Mother Box over her. He moved it in the air, from her toes up to her head.

While Mother Box hummed and pinged to herself, Himon told Diana that this, the first Mother Box, was his own invention. That Mother Boxes were activated by human will and connected to a cosmic power called the Source. That they could analyze and rearrange reality within a localized area.

Diana had noticed earlier that Himon treated his Mother Box not like a machine, but like a sentient being. And Himon assured her that, in a way, all Mother Boxes were alive.

Mother Box *ping-ping*ed and Himon asked her, "You're sure? And you can do nothing?"

She pinged again sadly.

Diana peered up at Himon anxiously. "How bad is it?"

"It doesn't get much worse," Himon said. "You have been implanted with a Brain Binder. At present, it is retrieving your memories and sending them . . . elsewhere."

"Elsewhere? You mean—to Desaad?" Diana began to feel sick.

"He must have implanted it while you were unconscious," Himon said. "The Binder is processing your memories, moving from the most recent to your most distant past. It can even retrieve memories you've lost or forgotten or were otherwise unaware of. When an especially intense or powerful memory is accessed, it triggers one of those trancelike flashbacks.

"The contents of your mind are being dissected and digitized," he continued. "And simultaneously Desaad will be rewriting the codes. If he recaptures you, he will wipe your mind and upload the counterfeit reality he has created. You will become one of Darkseid's creatures, with no memory of any other existence."

This was worse...so much worse...than Diana had imagined. All her life, she had hated being told what to do. Now she could become a zombie-like puppet incapable even of having the *thought* of disobedience. The shock left her gasping for air.

For an instant the world shrank to a dark tunnel. Then her Amazon training reasserted itself. She took deep, calming breaths. "Mother Box can't—?"

"Deactivate the implant? No, that can only be accessed through the primary equipment in Desaad's laboratory."

"But I'm safe—as long as I remain free?" Diana asked.

"Yes. I invented the Boom Tube technology, Diana," Himon said. "I could send you back to Earth."

Diana bit her lip. Oh, Great Hera, there was nothing she wanted more. Except—

"I can't!" she said. "I can't leave Apokolips without my armor."

Darkseid stood on a stone balcony, gazing over Apokolips. The Fire Pits sent light and shadow racing through the clouds and illuminated his stony countenance in strobelike flashes.

Watching from the doorway, the cringing Desaad rubbed his hands nervously and studied Darkseid's expression like an oracle trying to read the omens. How should he behave? How could he best redeem himself?

But, as usual, Darkseid's granite face revealed nothing.

"This Diana is indeed a Wonder Woman," Darkseid said. There was a silky edge to his voice that made Desaad shudder. "Even without her armor, she escaped your escape-proof prison, and has cut a swath across Apokolips—defeated Parademons, Dog Soldiers, aerotroopers, Female Furies, the Brain Bound—even your own sister, Bernadeth. She has survived magnificently the gauntlet of tests Apokolips has thrown at her.

"Once I am able to control her, Desaad, what a weapon she will make!"

Desaad sighed, relieved. All was not yet lost. He could salvage the situation. He allowed himself a sour smile. "The memory retrieval process is right on schedule, Sire. Soon we will recapture her and Bind her to your will."

"She has disappeared into the bowels of Armagetto," Darkseid said.

"With Himon's help, Sire!" Desaad was indignant.

"Himon! He has long been a thorn in my side!" Darkseid grumbled. "Reassure me, Desaad, you *do* have a plan to recapture Wonder Woman?"

Desaad cringed forward. "Yes, Sire! We will send troops into Armagetto. Punish the Lowlies! Take increasing numbers of them and let it be known that we will Bind them, to make *them* pay for Wonder Woman's escape and Himon's treason.

"That will draw your enemies from their hideout—and into our trap."

CHAPTER
15

For almost a day, Diana lay on a pallet in Himon's inaccessible chamber while her thoughts wore a track in her mind.

She had taken the magic armor from Athena's temple. It was bonded to her now, but was not hers. It belonged to the Amazons and she *had* to get it back.

But if she tried and failed and was recaptured...?

Darkseid would make her into a stealth weapon to destroy the Justice League. Without their protection, Earth itself would be in jeopardy.

Whether she acted or did nothing, her memories would continue to trickle into Desaad's computers, like sand through an hourglass. And they would lead Darkseid to Themyscira....

THE RACE

The race is almost over.

Diana and her young rivals have crossed fields, jumped culverts, splashed through streams, and are now approaching the cliff face. They have only to climb the cliff, retrieve the lambs tethered at its top, and race, carrying the animals across their shoulders, to the arena.

Diana is the youngest of the competitors, but she is tall for her age, and athletic. Despite her daughter's comparative youth, Hippolyta is expecting Diana to win.

And indeed, Diana is the first to reach the cliff and begin her climb. She is halfway up when she hears the terrified bleating.

She climbs desperately, fearing disaster. As she clears the top she sees the lambs tugging frantically at their tethers as a Harpy—a hideous monster with a woman's head and vulture's body—drags a lamb into the air. A dozen more monsters are wheeling above.

Diana hurls a rock at the Harpy, striking the monster's forehead. With a shriek of anger, it drops the lamb. Diana dives and catches it.

Two more young Amazons have reached the cliff top and are gaping up at the circling monsters.

Diana lobs another rock at the Harpies. "Hurry!" she tells the older girls. "We need to get the lambs away from here!"

"But the race!" her friend Iona says. "Grab your lamb and run! You're winning!"

"I don't care about winning!" Diana hurls another stone. "Just save the lambs."

"We could help drive those monsters off!" Kore says. But her rock falls short. The Harpies make rude noises.

"I throw hardest and fastest," Diana snaps. "Do what I say! It's the best way!"

Iona shrugs. "All right! We'll send reinforcements!"

They snatch up lambs and race down the mountain path as the rest of the contestants finally reach the cliff top.

The stones Diana has thrown have already knocked out several Harpies. She shouts to the other girls, "They're focused on me now! You'll be safe. Just take the lambs and run!"

When Hippolyta and the adult Amazons arrive, they find Diana standing protectively over a tiny lamb, battling a half dozen remaining Harpies.

The arrows of the Amazons soon drive the monsters away.

Diana watches as Iona receives the victory wreath. She's sorry to have disappointed her mother, but Diana smiles bravely and tells herself it doesn't matter; she lost the race but she's sure that what she did was right.

She just hopes Athena is pleased with her.

Even if she didn't win.

Diana jerked upright, her heart hammering. She had fallen into another memory, had become completely enmeshed in her younger self.

She had only been in training a few years then. She'd been so innocent. So trusting . . .

That night, Hippolyta brushes Diana's hair back from her tear-stained cheek and whispers, "You made the right choice, my child. Our people will remember this day and know that, in a crisis, you will choose

their safety before your own, and protect them as you did the lambs!"

Diana startled awake, fighting off the fog of trance. Was that a memory—or simply wishful thinking? Diana's thoughts tumbled confusedly.

When she was finally alone in her room in the palace, she *had* cried herself to sleep, but—? Had her mother really come into her room? Really said—? But if she had, surely Diana would have remembered. And not become so angry and resentful later.

It must be a true memory, she realized. After all, Himon had told her that the Binder could access memories she didn't even know she had.

Diana prowled the cavern, feeling as if the walls were closing in around her.

Finally, she asked Himon if there was any way she could disguise herself and go outside, if only for a little while. After all, who would notice one more wretch among the teeming Lowlies of Armagetto?

Seeing her agitation, Himon agreed—on the condition that he go with her. "In truth, after hearing your adventures so far, I wouldn't trust you to walk across a street without getting into trouble."

Diana smiled. She knew his joking only masked his concern that another memory would overwhelm her and she would inadvertently reveal herself to Desaad's minions.

Himon opened a cabinet and handed Diana a ragged tunic and leggings. "Put them on!" he told her.

Then he held Mother Box next to her face. "All right," he told her. "You're ready."

Diana looked puzzled.

Himon pulled a mirror from the cabinet. "Look!"

In the glass, Diana saw an ancient crone. She looked as wrinkled and bent as the old fisherman she had rescued. She put her hands to her cheeks and felt leathery furrows.

Himon winked. "As I told you, Mother Box can re-arrange reality!"

Then Mother Box altered Himon's appearance.

And together, Diana and Himon walked through the wall, into the corridors beyond, and out into the sulfurous stench of Armagetto.

This time, the streets teemed with Lowlies, desti-
tute and beaten down by life.

"Himon?" Diana asked.

He glanced toward her. "What is it?"

"Your invention—Mother Box—lets you phase
through walls, heal deadly wounds, and transform
reality in other ways. If you can do so much, can't
you help these poor people?"

Himon shook his head sadly. "On Apokolips,
Darkseid's will is supreme. I can do small things.
Nurture hope in those different few. Teach them to
dream. But I can only aid those who want my help."

His blue eyes twinkled. "Not that it's stopped me
from trying. I have been denounced to the authori-
ties . . . and escaped their prisons . . . more times than
you can count—"

Screams interrupted Himon's discourse. The rough
voices of Dog Soldiers and the crack of weapon fire
up ahead sent panicking Lowlies fleeing past them.

Himon drew Diana into a recessed doorway. "We'll
phase below if necessary," he murmured. "But first
let's see what's going on!"

The Lowlies were in full-fledged stampede away from the Dog Soldiers, who shoved, cuffed, and herded any they could catch into a pitiable, trembling cluster.

"All right! That's today's haul!" a tall man in a hood of mail shouted.

"Who's that?" Diana asked.

"He's called Wonderful Willik, believe it or not. He's the District Protector, Darkseid's main enforcer in Armagetto," Himon whispered.

Once they knew they were safe from capture, albeit temporarily, the remaining Lowlies crept back, eager for spectacle. Willik gave it to them.

"Citizens of Armagetto, you are hiding a traitor among you—Himon, who has aided the escaped prisoner, Diana, also known as Wonder Woman." Willik held up a picture of Diana, dressed in her armor, for the crowd to see. "Darkseid wants them both!

"Today, on Desaad's order, I seized fifty of you. Tomorrow I will take one hundred. The day after that, two hundred. You see how it progresses. Each day, until these criminals are in Desaad's hands, I will arrest twice as many Lowlies as the day before. These prisoners will be Brain Bound and set to work among the Fire Pits.

"But the ever-merciful Darkseid will allow you to buy your freedom. You have only to surrender Himon and Wonder Woman to me!"

"Oh, no!" Diana whispered. Horror choked her. Tears streaked down her cheeks. "Fifty...a hundred...two hundred...four hundred...eight hundred and into the thousands! Day after day, innocent, helpless victims—captured, tortured, Brain Bound because of me! Darkseid and Desaad and Willik—they're like the Harpies, living to rend and tear! I can't allow that to happen!"

Diana pushed her way into the crowd. "Stop!" she cried. "Set them free! I surrender!"

CHAPTER
16

Diana shoved through the crowd toward Wonderful Willik. The Lowlies hooted and jeered.

"I surrender," Diana repeated. "I am Wonder Woman!"

"And I'm Desaad's old granny!" Willik's slash of a mouth curled in a sneer. "Are you so eager, hag, to join the Brain Bound?"

Diana was puzzled. How could Willik not believe her? Then she remembered that Mother Box had disguised her.

Himon, also disguised, shouldered through the crowd. "Crazy old crone!" he muttered. "She's my mom...and she's already plenty Brain Bound...if you catch my drift. Just last week, she thought she was Darkseid's own mother, Tigra!"

Diana knew that if she explained about the disguises, Himon, too, would be captured.

Willik cuffed Diana, then shoved her into Himon's arms. "Keep the hag off the streets, Lowlie, or next time, we take her in, and you with her!"

Himon dragged Diana away from Willik and the jeering crowd and into a deserted alley. And phased them into the tunnel below.

In the safety of Himon's hideout, Mother Box restored their features.

Diana turned to Himon angrily. "Why did you stop me? I'm the one Desaad really wants. I can't let those people be Brain Bound in my place!"

Himon looked grave. "Even if Darkseid uses you against Earth and Themyscira?"

Diana turned pale. She realized what a mess she had almost made of things.

"Oh, Hera, you're right! I acted impulsively! But, Himon, how can I let so many people be destroyed because of me?" Diana had never felt so miserable. "No matter what I do, I betray someone. Here or on Earth, because of me, innocent lives will be lost!"

Himon frowned. "I have so far avoided a direct

battle with Darkseid and his minions. But your bravery moves me to reconsider.

"I can think of one way to do it all—to free the captured Lowlies. To get your armor back, destroy Desaad's record of your memories, even return you safely to Earth.

"My plan will sound mad. We will both be in great danger. But the end will outweigh the risks. If you can bring yourself to trust me!"

TRUST

Diana leans from a recessed window in the weaving room of her mother's palace. She is supposed to be spinning wool—a punishment for her most recent transgression involving a pot of glue and her nurse's hairbrush.

But Diana has put her spindle-whorl aside and is staring outside longingly, where the bright sun beckons and a light breeze spins tiny petals in springtime drifts of color and fragrance.

And thus she sees the elegant veiled figure stealthily approach a side entrance. Hippolyta herself opens the door, so Diana knows this meeting is both secret and important.

Then Diana hears them whisper her own name.

They will talk in the upstairs parlor, she thinks. And the courtyard is now empty.

She grabs the heavy grapevine that grows up the wall, swings carefully onto a cross-branch, and clambers, monkey-like, toward the second floor. There she hangs, silent, unseen, and shamelessly listening.

Hippolyta is talking about Diana. About how much she had wanted a daughter . . . a perfect little girl. How Diana is the moon and stars to her.

Diana's heart swells with pride, and she climbs closer, eager to hear more about how wonderful she is.

And then the queen says, "But she can be so difficult—"

The other woman laughs, and Diana recognizes her voice. Her mother's visitor is Athena, Goddess of Wisdom and War!

"She isn't a docile child, is she?" Athena says. "But gifted as she has been, what can you expect? I *imagine her intelligence and curiosity have her constantly in trouble?"*

Hippolyta sighs. "Not to mention her pride and strength of will. I worry sometimes. Did the gods gift her too richly?"

After a moment, Athena answers, "I understand your fears, Hippolyta. Godly gifts can be used for good or ill. Some of Diana's traits may seem misplaced in a child barely out of the nursery. But when she is older they will put her in good stead. If you can help her learn to control them. If so, she is destined for greatness. If not . . ."

Hippolyta says hesitantly, "Athena, I had the oddest dream. . . ." Then her voice sinks to a whisper.

Diana edges out onto a smaller branch, trying to hear. But the vine beneath her feet tears loose. She clings desperately to the upper branch, as her toes scrabble for purchase.

The adult voices stop. And Hippolyta looks out the window.

"Diana! What—?" She reaches over the sill, hauls Diana into the room, and hugs her close. "You could have fallen. You—"

Then Hippolyta's body stiffens and she thrusts

Diana back so she can look into her eyes. "You w
eavesdropping!"

Diana raises her chin. "You were talking about me!
If I didn't listen, how could I know what you were say-
ing? Am I really destined for greatness?"

Solemnly, Athena studies Diana's mutinous little
face. But her voice holds laughter. "Your truthful-
ness is commendable, Princess, though your manners
leave a bit to be desired. And greatness must be
earned."

"You wish to learn things, Diana? Excellent!"
Hippolyta scowls angrily. "Tomorrow you will begin to
study the arts of war, as well as the arts of peace. You
must learn to pick your battles. And know your friends
from your enemies."

Diana glances at Athena. Somehow she knows
Athena is a friend. But she definitely does not want to
spend her days being forced to study things she
doesn't want to know. She thrusts out her chin.

And Hippolyta meets Diana's obstinate expression
with a similar stubborn thrust of her own jaw.

"Trust me, Diana!" Hippolyta says, almost grimly.
"These are skills you will master . . . for your own good
and the good of us all."

l. And her mind returned to present-

"That's one of my earliest memories, lost to Desaad," Diana whispered. "We don't have much time."

Himon smiled comfortingly. "As I've learned, to my regret, one person alone can't save a world. But maybe two can—if we work together."

Diana looked at him.

On Apokolips, she had seen what Earth would become under Darkseid's control. She had experienced violence, cruelty, and betrayal. Was Himon truly different than the others? she wondered. Was he really a friend?

Yes! Diana realized. Himon, in his dedication to a cause she didn't fully understand, reminded her of her own mother. And Athena.

Himon asked again, "Will you trust me?"

Diana smiled. "With my life. We'll stop Darkseid—together."

CHAPTER
17

In his secret underground laboratory, Himon sat hunched over a magnifying lens, using tiny instruments to create a chain of computer chips that looked like a piece of dark string.

Diana leaned over his shoulder. "I give up," she said. "What are you making?"

Himon carefully picked up the strand. "This is a Channel Blocker. When we are captive in Desaad's laboratory, it will temporarily disrupt his Brain Binder electrodes and keep them from reprogramming your mind."

"When we're—what?" Diana stammered. This was not at all what she wanted to hear.

Himon handed her the filament. "Weave it among

the strands of your hair. I've included jammers to protect it from discovery."

Apprehensively, Diana did as Himon told her. Mixed with her hair, the filament was undetectable.

"Okay," she said warily. "What now?"

Diana and Himon, swathed in hooded cloaks, sauntered down the crowded main street of Armagetto. They were jostled by the throng, but otherwise ignored.

"You'd think with their lives riding on it, the Lowlies would be looking for us!" Diana whispered. "We're going to have a hard time getting captured if Willik's enforcers are this apathetic."

Not that she exactly *wanted* to be captured. She felt queasy at the very thought of what they had planned. But she would do what she had to.

"The Lowlies live in the moment," Himon told her. "They've learned not to think about tomorrow, since it always proves worse than today."

Diana and Himon walked, unchallenged, toward the Precinct House. Two enforcers stood outside.

Himon winked at Diana. "If we simply turn ourselves in, they may suspect a trick. So we'll make
them arrest us."

He pulled a fist-sized ball from his pocket, flipped a
switch on top, and lobbed it between the enforcers.
The ball exploded harmlessly with a dramatic burst
of smoke. The enforcer looked around.

"There! Get them!" he shouted.

The enforcers grabbed Diana and Himon, who put
up only a token fight.

They dragged them before Wonderful Willik, who
didn't question his good fortune. Desaad—and great
Darkseid himself—would reward him well for this
capture.

Willik ordered Diana shackled hand and foot. But
Himon they wrapped, from toes to chin, in a thick,
form-fitting metal tube, closed with straps of pad-
locked steel. A mesh dome enclosed his head. Oddly
enough, the guards' overly cautious treatment of
Himon increased Diana's confidence in his plan.

They loaded the prisoners onto a flatbed transport
and paraded them through the squalid streets of
Armagetto. Occasionally, the transport stopped and
Willik made a self-serving speech in which he praised
himself for his daring capture of these dangerous

criminals—just one more example of his concern for the safety of the people of Armagetto. The Lowlies cheered indifferently.

The transport left Armagetto with its roaring Fire Pits. It picked up speed as it entered the area called Long Shadow. As they approached Grey Borders and rumbled toward the planet's governmental capital, Parademon patrols flew escort.

And finally, they reached Desaad's palace.

Guards transported the prisoners to an upper floor and shoved them roughly into Desaad's lab.

Desaad was groveling before the main communication screen, where Darkseid's granite face loomed darkly. Desaad flicked a glance toward Diana and Himon, and Diana could tell he was relieved, "... as you see, Sire, they have arrived, just as I promised. First Wonder Woman, then Himon, will be Bound to you."

A series of view screens threw a flickering light over Desaad's terrible machineries. In a distant corner, Diana saw her armor and lasso. So far the plan was working. But what good were all her wondrous gifts when all that stood between herself and oblivion was a filament the thickness of a hair?

ATHENA'S GIFT

In the column-lined Temple of Athena, at the foot of Athena's majestic statue, the Goddess-Queen Hippolyta stands, holding her infant daughter, Diana. Other goddesses surround her, watching expectantly as the oracle casts Diana's birth augury.

The seeress dashes the bones of a lioness upon the floor, then kneels, studying their arrangement closely. She gasps and looks up at the goddesses apprehensively. And when she speaks, her voice quivers.

"Themyscira is under the protection of the gods of Olympus. But a time of crisis will come when gods may be set against gods. And the fate of all will rest in the hands of the Princess Diana."

Confused, dismayed, the goddesses whisper to each other: What does this disturbing prediction mean? Will they fight among themselves? Or will gods from other pantheons attack them? What part will this infant play?

Whatever the meaning of the prophecy, the god-desses decide, their own responsibility is clear. They must guarantee that Diana has the special abilities she will need to fulfill her destiny.

Hera, Queen of the Gods, steps forward first as is her right. Laying her hand upon the infant's head, she says, "My gift to her is pride."

Queen Hippolyta smiles. "A fitting gift, Hera. She must understand and cherish her unique value. In Diana's name, I thank you."

Aphrodite, Goddess of Love, kisses the forehead of the infant. "I give her grace," she says.

"She will be as beautiful as a sunrise," promises Eos, Goddess of the Dawn, as she gently strokes Diana's cheek.

Artemis, huntress and protector of children, smiles. "I give her intelligence. She must learn quickly. And have great understanding."

Persephone, who was forced to spend half her time in the underworld, gives her courage, "...for Diana, too, will face dark times and will have great need of it."

Demeter, bountiful Goddess of the Harvests, gives Diana "strength of body."

Hestia, Protectress of the Hearth, offers "strength of character."

"Strength of will is my gift to her," says grim Nemesis, bringer of retribution.

Harmonia, who brings reconciliation, smiles gently. "Beauty and strength and intelligence are empty attributes without compassion. Though she will be well-suited for war, her empathy for others will make her strive for peace."

Finally, all eyes turn curiously to Athena, Goddess of Wisdom and War.

Athena smiles. "Of war, she will have her fill. And I would give the child wisdom if I could, but true wisdom must be learned.

"Our foreknowledge has brought her extraordinary abilities, which have already changed the course of her life. Our further interference could warp her growth and distort the choices she might make.

"My gift is that Diana will grow up unaware of her destiny. Until the time is right, the details of this prophecy will fade from your minds. You will remember only her potential for greatness. And she will be free to discover her own path.

"Hippolyta alone will half-remember the prophecy,

as if it had come to her in a dream. For she will need to train—and sometimes to restrain—her exceptional daughter . . ."

"Athena could hide that memory from your gods, Wonder Woman, but not from me!" Desaad's crafty voice murmured in Diana's ear.

Awareness returned in a rush.

Another memory lost to Desaad, Diana realized. This one from her infancy, before she could even consciously remember. She had never been told of such a prophecy, of course. Athena's gift had spared her that. But it explained so much—

Desaad interrupted her tumbling thoughts. "The prophecy will soon be fulfilled, in a way none of your gods could have foreseen. Because of their gifts, you yourself will bring disaster to Themyscira—and to your world. Once you are Bound to Apokolips, you yourself will lead the New Gods of Apokolips into the domain of the Old."

Without ceremony, Desaad lifted the spherical Brain Binder helmet and clamped it roughly onto Diana's head.

CHAPTER
18

Within the helmet, Diana felt a movement like scrabbling bugs as electrodes automatically moved into position and attached themselves to her skull.

She shuddered and looked wildly at Himon, but he winked reassuringly.

I can do this! she told herself. *Himon says it will be okay. He wouldn't lie. I trust him!*

Desaad turned to Himon. "Observe, Himon. My Brain Binder has collected, and rewritten, this so-called Wonder Woman's memories. When I press this button, it will overwrite her true experiences with ones I have devised for her. And she will exist only as Darkseid's slave."

Desaad reached toward the computer console.

"Dear Athena," Diana prayed with what might well

have been her last independent thought. "Help us! Please help us all!"

With desperate eyes, she watched Desaad depress the button.

Diana stiffened, then relaxed. Her expression lost its terror and became still and impassive.

"Diana!" Himon screamed. "No! Nooooo!"

Desaad smiled without mirth. "You see how easy it is. One moment she is a vibrant Wonder Woman; the next, she is a shell of her former self, empty of all but obedience.

"Even now my master Darkseid waits as my computers compile an overview of her original memories, focusing on those critical to the overthrow of the Justice League and the conquest of Themyscira."

Desaad stared into Diana's unfocused eyes. *Yes*, he thought, *she has the zombie look of the Brain Bound.* But did he have total power over her? he wondered. He would need to test his control in increments.

First he ordered the two guards to stand beside the door with weapons pointed at Diana. Then he removed the Brain Binder helmet from her head and unshackled her hands and feet.

Diana stood unmoving.

So far so good, Desaad thought. *Now, for the next*

test. The woman had a horror of Brain Binding. Let us see if she will betray her one friend on Apokolips.

Desaad held out the helmet. "Wonder Woman, take the helmet and place it on Himon's head."

Diana carried the helmet to Himon. But when she began to lower it, the mesh covering Himon's head was in the way. She turned to Desaad and waited passively for further orders.

Desaad chuckled. "Guard, remove the mesh!"

One of the guards unlocked and removed the covering. Then, at Desaad's signal, he stepped back, returning to full alert.

"Continue," Desaad commanded Diana.

Himon tried to struggle, but the casing that sheathed his body held him immobile as Diana lifted the helmet and placed it on his head.

Desaad smiled, satisfied. "If it were up to me, Himon, I would immediately obliterate your mind. But Lord Darkseid dislikes waste and has commanded me to withdraw your memories intact. He believes they hold technological possibilities.

"But as a precaution, during the Withdrawal process you will wear the helmet. Despite my Master's . . . preference, at your slightest move to escape, I will remove that possibility. Have no doubt,

Himon, when I am done, one way or the other, you will serve Apokolips, body and soul."

"I have always served Apokolips," Himon said coldly.

Desaad sneered. "When I am through, you will understand that to serve Apokolips is to serve the great Darkseid—for Darkseid and Apokolips are one!"

During this interchange, Diana waited quietly.

Pleased with her utter impassivity and his obvious control of her, Desaad went to the corner and picked up the armored breastplate. *Even without her armor, she is strong,* he thought. *But with it, she rivals the mightiest of the New Gods. To command such power...*

Desaad knew he should wait for the final test, let Darkseid himself be the one to master her, but Desaad's urge to dominate her was irresistible.

He handed Diana the armor. "Put it on," he ordered.

"I must make sure her bond with the armor wasn't compromised by the Binding process," he said to the guards. "Keep your weapons trained on her. And if she does anything she is not ordered to do, kill her."

Diana stood before Desaad, wearing the breastplate. She slipped on first one silver bracelet, and then the other. She picked up the unbreakable lasso and snapped it into the loop at her waist.

The guards, watching Diana through their weapon sights, were awestruck by that vision of beauty and power.

Even in her rags, Diana had been lovely. But garbed as Wonder Woman, she was magnificent. Her long, dark hair hung down her back in sumptuous waves. Her armor caught and reflected the lights of Desaad's lab and dazzled their eyes.

But her face remained expressionless and her body retained the submissive posture of the Brain Bound.

Reveling in his authority, Desaad ordered Diana to rise slowly into the air.

Immediately she rose. At Desaad's command, she flew slowly, first to the left, then to the right, finally drifting over the heads of the dazzled guards who trained their weapons on her.

Then, faster than they could react, she was dropping behind them, kicking out, simultaneously catching both guards at the base of their skulls. As they fell forward, unconscious, she grabbed their weapons and fired them into the Brain Binding computer.

"No!" Desaad shouted. "You're Brain Bound! That's impossible!"

He reached toward an alarm button. But Wonder Woman was there first, grabbing him by the hood and hurling him across the room.

Desaad slammed into the wall and slid down, unconscious.

Wonder Woman pulled the Brain Binder helmet from Himon's head and hurled it to the floor. Then she stomped down on it hard, crushing it beneath her foot.

"Your filament worked, Himon. My mind was protected. My will is my own!" she said as she ripped apart the metal shell that imprisoned him.

Himon stepped free. "If being a super hero ever fails, you could become a fine actress," he said. "You had me worried, despite our plan."

Wonder Woman smiled sadly. "I have seen the Brain Bound up close, so I knew how to mimic them."

Methodically, she smashed Desaad's machines, especially the computers that held her digitized memories. "Themyscira and the Earth are safe at last," she said.

Diana glanced at the wall screens displaying the dungeon cells.

"Now let's free Desaad's prisoners," she said as she walked toward the lab door.

CHAPTER

19

"**W**ait! The cells can be opened via a master switch," Himon said. He depressed a large lever. "There!"

On the observation screens, Wonder Woman could see cell doors sliding open. Slowly, prisoners began to shuffle forward, then run toward the exits. Wonder Woman knew the escapees would soon be climbing up the stairs as she had, searching for a way out. And Desaad's guards would be waiting for them.

"I've got to protect the Lowlies," she said, "until they're safely away from here."

Wonder Woman and Himon ducked out the lab door and sprinted down the hall toward the stairs.

Several guards rounded a corner and Wonder Woman drop-kicked them, hardly breaking stride.

She opened the stairwell door. From below came screams, shouts, the pop of weapon fire, and the tramping of hundreds of feet as they climbed up the stairs.

"The ground floor is three flights down," Himon said. "There's a side entrance that leads to the court-yard you escaped into."

On the ground floor, Wonder Woman threw open the stairwell door.

Guards and officers fired energy blasts, which she deflected with her miraculous silver bracelets. She ducked back into the stairwell.

"Wait here!" she said to Himon. "I'll be right back."

Wonder Woman flew down a corridor, evading and deflecting weapon fire and taking out the attacking guards and officers.

She ripped the exterior door from its hinges and smashed a gaping hole in the courtyard wall.

Then she zoomed back inside.

Wonder Woman flew down the stairwell.

She assailed the guards, deflected their weapon fire, and protected the Lowlies as they streamed past her up the stairs toward freedom.

They ran like frightened animals, not stopping to glance her way or thank her. Not questioning their good fortune. Only scrabbling desperately for safety.

So Wonder Woman was amazed when a teenage boy hesitated and looked up. The crowd almost knocked him down, and he fought to stand upright as he shouted up at her. "I thought we Lowlies were too worthless for anyone to care about. But I was wrong. Thank you!"

An old woman behind him grunted and shoved. "Stop jawing and move, boy. We ain't free yet!"

On the landing leading to the ground floor, Himon waited. The teenager stepped away from the Lowlies streaming past and stood looking at Himon with shining eyes. "You're a legend among us, sir. I hope I see you again."

"You will, lad, that I promise," Himon told him. "Mother Box will lead me to you."

The boy smiled shyly at Himon. Then he ran out the door and into the slums beyond.

The last of the prisoners was dashing to freedom as Wonder Woman rejoined Himon on the landing. Seeing his smile, she asked, "You spoke with that boy?"

"He's beginning to know his own value," Himon told her. "And his eyes will open to myriad possibilities."

Mother Box pinged several times, interrupting them.

"Mother Box tells me Desaad had back-up equipment. But, while we were in his lab, she was able to trace and analyze their frequencies. She has just created and broadcast a virus that, even now, is destroying every Brain Binder program on Apokolips."

Desaad's sneering voice came from the stairwell above. "You were fools to risk recapture and death to free those ingrate Lowlies. And even greater fools to think you could foil me so easily. Guessing what you would do, I have already taken measures to reacquire an intact Brain Binder program. Your efforts there were wasted."

Wonder Woman glanced at Himon, alarmed. "What—?"

"He's probably referring to the canister still on Earth. It would contain intact Brain Binder technology."

"Twenty points!" Desaad sneered.

Wonder Woman grabbed Desaad by the front of his robe. "What have you done?"

Desaad smirked. "Invisible though it remains, your Justice League cohorts found the canister and took it to their satellite headquarters. Minutes back, I transported a squad of Parademons there to retrieve it."

From outside Desaad's manor, Wonder Woman could hear shouted commands and running footsteps.

Desaad smiled. "It seems that, while we stood chatting, my Master and his troops arrived. I anticipate your recapture—"

Wonder Woman snarled, "Then you're doomed to disappointment!" She threw Desaad roughly against the wall. He slid to the ground, once again unconscious.

"Himon," she said. "You once told me you could send me back to Earth. Can you send me to our satellite instead?"

"Place the coordinates in your mind," Himon told

her. "Mother Box will call up a Boom Tube and deliver you there."

Wonder Woman took his hands in hers. "Thank you, Himon—and Mother Box—for this and for all you have done."

As she stepped back, Himon smiled gently. "And I thank you, Wonder Woman. You have given an old man hope. You are a woman of spiritual as well as physical strength, worthy of your armor. Now leave! We must both be gone before Lord Darkseid arrives."

She hesitated. "You can get away safely, then?"

Himon grinned mischievously. "That shouldn't be a problem!" Mother Box *ping-pinged* and Himon began to fade into invisibility.

Then Wonder Woman heard a clap of thunder as the Boom Tube vortex surrounded her, teleporting her back toward Earth.

CHAPTER
20

Wonder Woman fell from the Boom Tube onto the main observation deck of the Watchtower—the Justice League's satellite headquarters. Behind her, the teleportation vortex disappeared.

Through the large floor-to-ceiling window, Diana saw the planet Earth orbiting below and spotted the Aegean Sea, where Themyscira lay hidden by the magic of the ancient gods she served. *Please, Athena, help me keep them safe!* she prayed silently.

Strident sounds of battle clamored behind her. She whirled and saw a tangle of warring figures and ricocheting energy blasts, a cacophony of grunts and shouts, of screams of anger and shrieks of pain.

She sighed with relief. *If the battle's still going on,*

I'm not too late, she thought. *They haven't got the canister. Yet.*

She spotted Superman using heat vision to melt Parademon weapons into slag. Then Superman himself was hidden by a swarm of attackers.

As Wonder Woman rushed to aid him, she heard the crunch of knuckles on demon-flesh. She ducked as an unconscious Parademon sailed overhead and slammed into the viewport window. She dodged a second, and a third, till she reached Superman and joined the fray.

Superman's voice was warm with relief. "Diana! It's good to have you back!"

She started to ask him where the League had stored the canister, then held her tongue. If the Parademons didn't know, she didn't want to help them find out.

A group of Parademons tackled her, knocking her into Martian Manhunter, who abruptly disappeared. The Parademon attackers rose in gawking, squawking confusion.

"Green devil was just here!"

"Where'd he go?"

Invisible hands pulled off several of the monsters,

freeing Wonder Woman. And invisible fists began to pummel them in earnest, with a strength that rivaled Superman's.

"Useful power," she said. "Thanks, Manhunter!"

"My pleasure," said his voice. "Welcome home!"

Down a corridor, a beam of emerald energy was surging from the Power Ring wielded by Green Lantern. By an act of will, Green Lantern had shaped the ring's energy into a cage that had imprisoned a score of Parademons.

Hawkgirl, hovering at his back, swung her mace with eager expertise, knocking aside their attackers. A pile of fallen Parademons attested to her skill and strength.

The Flash was racing at superspeed, skillfully evading ricocheting energy and tricking Parademons into firing blasts at him that inevitably struck their own comrades.

Wonder Woman saw that, for now, her teammates were more than holding their own. Except—where was Batman?

Batman, the only member of the Justice League without superpowers, was a hero by dint of talent and determination, but most of all, through force of intellect. He would have *deduced* what Wonder Woman knew: that this attack, this pitched battle was a diversion to distract the Justice League while other Parademons searched the Watchtower for the canister.

Batman would have rushed to protect it.

She grabbed at the Flash as he went by. "The canister, Flash! Where is it?"

Grinning, the Flash screeched to a halt. "Hey, Princess! You're back!" Then he looked at her blankly. "What canister?"

"The one that—" she began, then realized she couldn't go there. So she asked instead, "Where's Batman?"

Flash glanced around, concerned. "I don't know. His lab maybe? He was in there working on that invisible thing you—"

So the canister's still invisible, she thought. She didn't know if that was good or bad, but at least she knew where to find it.

"*That's* why the Parademons are here!" she whispered urgently. "Tell the others! Hurry! I'll help Batman!"

She flew down the maze of corridors to Batman's laboratory. Dismayed to see that the lab door had been forced open, she rushed inside.

Parademons, felled by Batman's assorted inventive weaponry, lay among the shattered remains of modern scientific equipment. Batman himself, scored by a dozen wounds, was fighting several monsters hand to hand.

Even as Wonder Woman dove to aid him, one of the fallen Parademons fired a blast, striking Batman in the shoulder. He collapsed sideways across a counter, but his body was suspended above its surface by . . . a *thing* that wasn't there!

With a shout of triumph, his Parademon assailants spotted their objective and lunged for the invisible cylinder. But Wonder Woman was there before them. She snatched the canister into her arms, leapt high into the air, and kicked out. The Parademons flew backward and slammed into several others.

But at their cries, other Parademons had swarmed into the lab.

Wonder Woman reeled backward under their onslaught. Tucking the invisible canister beneath one arm, she used the bracelet on the other to deflect their weapon blasts.

Though she fought desperately, she knew that she alone could not prevail against such numbers. Several of the monsters had already gotten close enough to tug at the invisible cylinder, and she could feel it slipping.

Then, in a burst of heat, the Parademons tumbled backward. With the Flash in the lead, Superman, Green Lantern, and the rest of the Justice League poured into the lab.

The room became a maelstrom of fists and fangs, of wings and weapon blasts.

And when it was over, not a single Parademon was left standing.

Diana knelt beside Batman. He opened his eyes and smiled up at her. "You showed up in the nick of time!" he said. "Any idea what's in that . . . invisible cylinder?"

As they tended Batman's flesh wounds, Wonder Woman told the League about her adventure on Apokolips, of the threat that Darkseid's Brain Binder posed, and of Himon's help in neutralizing that problem. Only the canister on Earth had remained a threat. Superman lifted the invisible cylinder and smiled grimly. "It won't be a threat after I throw it into the sun," he said. "Not even Apokoliptian technology can survive that!"

Green Lantern grumbled, "All this has been...interesting, Wonder Woman. But next time you might consider sticking to the plan!"

Wonder Woman grinned. "You know, GL, I just might *do* that!"

She glanced at the corner of the room where the unconscious and disarmed Parademons had been neatly stacked, and wrinkled her nose with disgust. "What are we going to *do* with all these Parademons?"

With a roar, a Boom Tube appeared, swept up the Parademons, and was gone.

Superman quirked a brow. "Apparently Desaad didn't want us questioning his minions too closely."

"Desaad might not work and play well with others," she said, suppressing her laughter, "but at least he picks up his toys when he's finished playing with them."

On Apokolips, Desaad was hunched disconsolately in his destroyed lab. He was so miserable he hardly cringed as his master Darkseid swept into the room, then stopped abruptly, surveying the wreckage.

Darkseid's granite brow lifted sardonically. "Wonder Woman did all this? Freed all your prisoners? And then escaped?"

"With Himon's help!" Desaad muttered savagely. "I had the Brain Binder on his head. I was so close to destroying him."

"It wouldn't have worked," Darkseid said. "Even if I had allowed it. Theirs was a bold stratagem, Desaad. They practically forced Willik to arrest them. And they came here *prepared* to destroy your hold on Wonder Woman. I suppose we have lost all the Wonder Woman data?"

Desaad cringed. "Every shred of it! I ran the Amazon through the gauntlet that is Apokolips, Sire. I tested her. But, in the end, I failed to deliver the data. Or her—Brain Bound—to you! Forgive me!"

Darkseid shrugged. "An interesting experiment, Desaad. But I hardly need Brain Binding to dominate Apokolips—or Earth!"

Wonder Woman's achievements were most impressive, Darkseid thought, *even in befriending the only man on Apokolips who could have helped her. Perhaps, in this Amazon, I have finally found a goddess who is worthy of me.*

Aboard the Watchtower, the Justice League sat down to dinner. They raised their glasses in a toast to Himon.

The Flash said, "To the most godly New God on Apokolips!"

He glanced sideways at Wonder Woman, waiting for her to mention Amazons, or remind him that her mother was a goddess or that she knew a batch of *real* gods.

But she didn't do any of those things.

She simply clinked glasses with him and smiled.

Wonder Woman stood alone on the observation deck, studying the Earth below.

After seeing Apokolips, Diana finally understood that it was Hippolyta's love of Themyscira's peace and beauty—and superior understanding of what might one day happen to her realm—that had made her train her daughter as a champion against such evil.

Diana was grateful now for her education. Because of that training, she had grown into the warrior that she needed to become.

Diana silently thanked the wise Athena, whose gift had let her grow up headstrong instead of simply burdened with duty. Because she had been given the ⟨…⟩m to follow her heart, when the time came for her to act, she was able to take the armor—though it was forbidden—and thus fulfill her birth prophecy.

Diana hoped that, one day, Hippolyta would understand that and forgive her for leaving their island home. But Diana knew that, in using her special skills to protect the whole Earth, she had made the right choice.

And whatever happened, Diana also knew, she would always be an Amazon.

ABOUT THE AUTHOR

LOUISE SIMONSON was born in Atlanta, where she attended Georgia State University. Her first job in comics was at Warren Publishing, where she eventually became vice president and senior editor. At Marvel Comics she was an editor of numerous titles, including *Star Wars* and *The Uncanny X-Men*. Simonson left her editorial position to pursue a freelance writing career, creating the award-winning *Power Pack* series. Among other titles she has written are *X-Factor*, *The New Mutants*, and *Web of Spider-Man*. For DC Comics she has scripted *Batman*, *The New Titans*, and *Superman: Man of Steel*. She is also the author of *Superman: Doomsday & Beyond* (Bantam, 1993), *I Hate Superman!* (Little, Brown, 1996), and *Steel* (Troll, 1997), a novelization of the film starring Shaquille O'Neal, based on the character she co-created. She has also written numerous episodes of *The Multipath Adventures of Superman* (presented by Warner Bros. Online, 1999–2002). Louise Simonson lives in upstate New York with her husband, Walter, who is also a writer and artist.